There she was, pus

"Wouldn't it be easier to go with you?" Chris asked.

"People will get the wrong idea."

"So what? Eventually they're going to know we had sex. You said it yourself. Showing up together makes it look as if there was more to it than a one-nighter. Unless there's another reason why you don't want me around?"

Lizzie blushed.

"Is there another reason, Lizzie?"

"Like what?" She lifted her chin and he saw the spark of defiance in her eyes. He liked it. Liked her when she got a little fired up. She'd been this way before, too. A little on edge. Exciting.

He moved closer, saw her pupils widen, and that's when he knew. The cool, calm demeanor wasn't completely real. Oh, he had no doubt that she wanted it to be, but it wasn't. Another step put him directly in front of her, close enough that he could smell the light floral scent of her shampoo, see the way her pulse beat heavily at her throat.

"What are you doing?" she whispered.

"Shh," he ordered as he contemplated his next move.

Dear Reader,

Welcome to the Texas Rodeo Barons miniseries! I'm so thrilled to be kicking it off with *The Texan's Baby,* a story about how sometimes the things we need most happen when we least expect it—and don't recognize it either. That happens for Lizzie Baron when she crosses paths with Christopher Miller. That evening changes both their lives forever. At first it seems like their chance encounter turns their worlds upside down, but before long it's clear that this accidental pregnancy really is a blessing in disguise.

I'm new to the Harlequin American line, and when change happens it can be a teensy bit scary. It can also be wonderful, and over the past months I've met and gotten to know many of the authors of this amazing line. Every single one has been welcoming and generous and down-to-earth. I got to meet several of them in person in Atlanta in the summer of 2013, and our wonderful editors, too. I have to say, I think I landed in clover! Working with the other authors on this project has been a fabulous experience. They write from their hearts, and the women behind the words are just as warm and friendly as the stories they write.

I hope you enjoy Lizzie and Chris's story, and come back for the other great titles in the series, starting with Trish Milburn's *The Texan's Cowgirl Bride,* out next month!

Happy reading,

Donna

THE TEXAN'S BABY

DONNA ALWARD

⟨H⟩ **HARLEQUIN**® AMERICAN ROMANCE®

Special thanks and acknowledgment are given to Donna Alward for her contribution to the Texas Rodeo Barons continuity.

Recycling programs
for this product may
not exist in your area.

ISBN-13: 978-0-373-75523-3

THE TEXAN'S BABY

Copyright © 2014 by Harlequin Books S.A.

Printed in U.S.A.

www.Harlequin.com

ABOUT THE AUTHOR

A busy wife and mother of three (two daughters and the family dog), Donna Alward believes hers is the best job in the world: a combination of stay-at-home mom and romance novelist. An avid reader since childhood, Donna has always made up her own stories. She completed her arts degree in English literature in 1994, but it wasn't until 2001 that she penned her first full-length novel and found herself hooked on writing romance. In 2006 she sold her first manuscript, and now writes warm, emotional stories for Harlequin.

In her new home office in Nova Scotia, Donna loves being back on the east coast of Canada after nearly twelve years in Alberta, where her career began, writing about cowboys and the West. Donna's debut romance, *Hired by the Cowboy,* was awarded a Booksellers' Best Award in 2008 for Best Traditional Romance.

With the Atlantic Ocean only minutes from her doorstep, Donna has found a fresh take on life and promises even more great romances in the near future!

Donna loves to hear from readers. You can contact her through her website, www.donnaalward.com, or follow @DonnaAlward on Twitter.

Books by Donna Alward

HARLEQUIN AMERICAN ROMANCE
1485—HER RANCHER RESCUER*

HARLEQUIN ROMANCE
4240—HONEYMOON WITH THE RANCHER
4251—A FAMILY FOR THE RUGGED RANCHER
4270—HOW A COWBOY STOLE HER HEART
4311—THE LAST REAL COWBOY
4317—THE REBEL RANCHER
4347—SLEIGH RIDE WITH THE RANCHER
4368—LITTLE COWGIRL ON HIS DOORSTEP*
4384—A COWBOY TO COME HOME TO*
4401—A CADENCE CREEK CHRISTMAS*

*Cadence Creek Cowboys

Other titles by this author available in ebook format.

To Trish, Barbara, Pamela, Cathy, and Tanya—for making this newbie feel at home.

Chapter One

Two minutes and thirty-three seconds to go.

Lizzie Baron stared at her watch with dismay. It had only been twenty-seven seconds since she started the timer on her watch. She refused to look until the full three minutes was up. Instead she checked her reflection in the mirror of the executive bathroom of the Baron Energies offices. She brushed a flake of mascara off the crest of her cheek and tucked a strand of rebellious hair behind her ear. She smoothed her skirt—a straight, businesslike skirt in boring charcoal-gray that ended just a shade above her knee, and checked the buttons of her matching fitted jacket for stray threads.

Perfect.

One minute, seventeen seconds.

Three minutes had never, ever in the history of the world, been this long. She was sure of it.

Her stomach churned uneasily but she told herself it was just nerves. Stress. She worked long hours at her job and didn't get much downtime. Everyone at Baron was on edge since they had recently lost a major contract in the Gulf. The tension level in the downtown Dallas office could be cut with a knife most days. Stress could definitely have caused her period to be late, right?

Except, a little voice inside her head reminded her,

*your period was due before that particular piece of bad
news, remember?*

Twenty-six seconds.

She breathed in and out. She was not pregnant. It
wasn't possible. Well, it was. Technically. But highly im-
probable. She didn't have time for this. And a one-night
stand with a rodeo bum…well, how often did people get
pregnant from one night?

She smiled grimly at the reflection of her face, her
skin oddly pale under the unflattering fluorescent lighting. The answer to that was simple. It *always* only took
one time for someone to get pregnant. Granted, the
chances went up with frequency of… She swallowed.
They hadn't exactly slept a lot that night.

Zero seconds.

Lizzie took a deep breath. Putting off looking wouldn't
change the result. She reached for the stick and stared at
the little window.

A plus sign.

She was pregnant.

Just flipping wonderful.

LIZZIE GOT OUT of her car, blinking in the brightness of
the San Antonio sun. She'd used the almost four-hour
drive to prepare, to work out what she was going to say.
The first thing she'd done after taking the home test
was visit the doctor, where her pregnancy had been confirmed. Lizzie hadn't wanted to say anything to anyone
until she was 100 percent sure the first test hadn't been a
false positive. Her mind was still reeling with the news,
and she was trying to sort out how she was going to tell
her family.…

They were going to seriously freak. And be disappointed. Who, in this day and age, went around having

sex with strangers? She bit down on her lip. She was a joke. A statistic. A casualty of the 1 percent of condoms that failed at a crucial moment.

She'd always felt like the responsible one. When Delia Baron left her kids, Brock had been on his own, and Lizzie had stepped in and mothered her younger siblings. Then her dad had married Peggy and adopted her boys, Jacob and Daniel. Those years had been pretty good. They'd all lived together out at Roughneck Ranch—the name a deliberate hat-tip to the oil industry that had put the Baron name on the map. Lizzie had cared for Peggy a lot, which meant Peggy's death had been especially hard to take.

Now her father was married again, this time to a much younger wife. Lizzie might have resented Julieta, who was only ten years older than herself, except Lizzie had found an unexpected friend and support in her step-mother.

Telling her would probably be the easiest of the family. Julieta never judged. She was always after Lizzie to get out and enjoy life more. Lizzie was fairly sure, though, that this wasn't what Julieta meant.

For one night only she'd allowed herself to cut loose. What a fool she'd been for thinking she could work out her frustrations by being so self-indulgent, that she could be irresponsible without repercussions and consequences. It was totally out of character.

But sometimes she felt as though she was the one who took on all the heavy lifting in the family, was the rock for all her brothers and sisters when they went through stuff. She was tired of being Lizzie who never made mistakes, Lizzie who did everything right. Lizzie, Brock Baron's firstborn.

Yeah, Jacob was pretty much the same age as she was,

but he was her stepbrother. Lizzie was the oldest and her brother Jet was the baby. Sometimes she wished they were reversed in the birth order, because Brock wouldn't give up the idea that Jet would take over Baron Energies one day. Problem was Jet wasn't remotely interested.

Lizzie, on the other hand, had missed out on her fun years because she had been too busy getting her education and stepping into a role at the family company. She was supposed to set an example.

It was a lot of pressure.

Lizzie sighed and shut the car door, feeling the heat of the sun soak through her tailored jacket. What she really needed was a coffee. A nice, big, strong coffee with two sugars and real cream. Sadly, since the moment the test was positive, she'd given up the caffeine and cut back on the sugar. The result had been three days of caffeine withdrawal headache and irritability.

And through it all one thought had stuck in her brain. Lizzie needed to talk to *him*. The baby's father.

There was no question about that. Christopher Miller deserved to know the truth and deserved to hear it from her—not from anyone else. What if the media got a hold of the story? They'd been quick to report the lost contract in the biz pages, and she already felt extra scrutiny from all sides as she sat at the boardroom table. Only thirty and vice president of a major energy corporation—not to mention being the boss's daughter. The old boys' club was just waiting for her to screw up.

Besides, it wasn't like she was going to be able to hide her condition forever. She was already almost eight weeks along. Another couple months and she'd be showing. It would be far better to do damage control right now and get on with things.

She looked up at the attractive stucco condos and

wished there was a way to make this look like less of a disaster. But no matter how she spun it, the bald truth remained. She'd been stupid. Impulsive. She'd let the family down—especially her dad. She knew how it would look to the shareholders and the press.

Mark Baker, Baron's CFO, would practically be crowing about it. He was dying to get his chance to be in the driver's seat at Baron, urging Brock to retire. It burned her biscuits that he might have any leverage on her, the pompous jerk.

Her headache was starting to come back, so she made her way over to one of the low stone walls by the building where there was some shade under a sycamore tree. All she had to do was remember her plan. Plans were good. Plans were soothing. Plans gave the illusion of control in the midst of chaos.

She gathered herself together and walked purposefully to the front door of the building, stepping into a blessedly cool air-conditioned foyer. The second set of doors was locked for security, so she scanned the panel of residents for his name. There it was—C. Miller, unit 406. She pressed the buzzer and waited.

As the seconds ticked past, she looked around. The complex was quite nice. The buildings were well kept, the grass cut neatly and urns of flowering plants flanked the entrance. It was definitely not what she'd expected from the dusty bronc rider she'd met two months ago. He wasn't that high up in the standings, either, so how on earth did he afford this place? Momentarily she wondered if she'd gotten the wrong Christopher Miller. What if she'd come all this way for nothing?

There was a click and then a voice. "Hello?"

Something stirred inside her at the sound of his voice. It was just one word but it was familiar—the low grit of it skimming over her nerve endings. She swallowed. "Uh…hi. I'm looking for Christopher Miller?"

"That's me."

"It's…uh…" She scrambled to think of what she'd said to him that night. How much she'd revealed. *Plans,* she reminded herself. *Just stick to the script.* "It's Elizabeth."

There was a pause.

"From the bar in Fort Worth."

The words came out strained.

"Come on up. Elevator's through the doors and to the left."

There was a click—and a buzzing sound as he let her in.

She pulled open the door and stepped inside. The tiled floor of the lobby gleamed as if freshly waxed and potted trees were spaced throughout the small area. There was a small table flanked by two chairs to the right, adding a homey yet classy touch. An elevator waited and she pushed the up arrow button. Seconds later the door opened and she stepped inside the car.

She could do this. She could see him and speak to him in a businesslike way and explain what she intended to do. She didn't need anything from him. Didn't *want* anything from him. He was completely and utterly off the hook.

The doors slid open at the fourth floor and she ran her hands down her skirt and then over her hair, making sure the knot at the back was smooth and neat. Stepping out, she started down the hallway. Number 401 was on the left, 402 on the right. Two more doors to go. She would knock. Smile. Begin with "you must be surprised to see me…"

A door opened and Christopher stepped into the hall. Her feet halted and she stared at him awkwardly, her practiced words flying out of her head. She'd definitely gotten the right guy. Around six feet, with dark hair that curled around his collar and gorgeous chocolaty eyes that crinkled in the corners. He wore jeans and a T-shirt but was in his bare feet, and his hair was glistening, as though he'd recently got out of the shower. Oh boy.

He was staring at her, too, like she was a stranger. "It really is you," he said, shaking his head a little. A wrinkle formed between his eyebrows. "What the hell are you doing here?"

For weeks, Chris had been wondering if he should try to find out who she was. She'd only said her name was Elizabeth. They'd met at a honky-tonk in Fort Worth after a less-than-stellar rodeo performance on his part. She'd been sitting at the bar, sipping a beer right from the bottle. His first impression had been surprise. Despite wearing jeans and boots and a T-shirt, there was a look of class about her. She looked more the wine-and-cheese type rather than beer and chips.

He'd had a good first round that weekend, but then he'd drawn Devil's Spawn. The horse was aptly named, it turned out, because Chris had been launched into the stratosphere in the second round after 4.6 seconds. He'd missed out on the money. No buckle bunnies had followed him to the bar and that had been just fine with him. He'd figured he'd nurse his wounds with a beer and head back to the motel where he was staying. Take a hot bath to soothe his sore muscles.

And then he'd seen her. He'd ordered another beer, looked over at her and she'd smiled, a soft little smile, and all his brain cells turned to mush.

When he'd woken the next morning, the bed had been

empty. The only evidence that she'd been there was the earring she'd left behind. How very cliché.

That had been nearly two months ago. Since then he'd done better, hitting the finals in a few rodeos, bringing in a little cash to help cover his expenses. It wasn't like this was his livelihood or anything. He was only on a leave of absence from his regular job. A job which had suddenly felt very claustrophobic after years of long hours. He missed the outdoors, missed the horses and the thrill. Missed having *fun*.

This leave of absence was his one last chance. Not that he expected to earn any titles. He'd been out too long and he was getting older. Another few years and he wouldn't be quite so resilient. If he were going to relive his youth one last time, it had to be now…before he lost his nerve. So he'd have no regrets. One last chance to live the life he wanted rather than the one that was expected of him.

Now *she* was here, standing not ten feet away. Forget the jeans and boots, too. She was the picture of elegance and power, moderately tall and slim, and wore her dark hair up in a conservative knot rather than the long, sexy ponytail he remembered. A great pair of legs was shown to excellent advantage in a slim skirt and sexy black heels. Buckle bunny? Not in a million years. The woman before him now was used to being in charge. If it weren't for the stunning blue eyes, she'd barely resemble the woman he remembered from the motel that night.

Something curled through him and his pulse took a strange hop as an image flashed through his mind. Her hair had been down, spread over the pillow and her smile had been sexy and more than a little naughty as she reached up and grabbed the collar of his shirt, pulling him down on top of her. What the hell was she doing in San Antonio now, looking like she did?

"Elizabeth," he said quietly, stepping aside so she could enter his apartment. He didn't have a good feeling about her showing up unannounced.

"Call me Lizzie." She gave him a faint smile and slid into the apartment ahead of him, taking care not to touch him in any way, he noticed. "Everybody does."

"You didn't say your name was Lizzie the night we met." He followed her inside and shut the door. She looked at him nervously, pulling her hands together.

"I was trying to be mysterious."

"It worked." He put his hands in his pockets. "How did you find me?"

Was that a bit of color in her pale cheeks? Her gaze skittered away slightly and her fingers twisted tighter together. "I tried 411 first, but there are over one hundred Christopher Millers in the state of Texas."

He waited for her to go on.

She frowned. "So then I tried Google. I entered your name and added '+ saddle bronc' to the search. San Antonio popped up. But there's more than one Christopher Miller here, too. So I called a friend of mine, called in a favor, and they gave me your address."

"A friend?"

"Yeah." She tried a small smile. "Rodeo's a small world. Which was why I was surprised that I'd never heard of you before."

His hands came out of his pockets. "You're saying that you got my address from rodeo records?"

The blush was back. "Yes."

He wasn't sure if that information was guaranteed to be confidential or not; he'd never considered it either way. But Elizabeth—Lizzie—had gone to some trouble to find him. He was pretty sure the reason wasn't going to be a good thing. She didn't look like she was the type to come out with "I couldn't forget our night together."

That sounded snide in his mind and more than a little hypocritical, since he hadn't been able to forget that night one bit. And if he'd had more to go on than a first name, he might have gone looking for her, too.

"Why would you do that?"

She straightened her shoulders and unclenched her hands. "Because I need to talk to you."

Quiet settled through the condo. This was so bizarre. Not what he expected in the middle of the day. Hell, he was only in town today to do some laundry and pack his duffel before heading back out to his mom and dad's. She was lucky to have caught him.

She definitely hadn't shown up bent on seduction. Everything about her screamed *hands off.* Just his bad luck he found that crazy sexy. Not that he planned on trying anything, but her tidy suit and librarian hair fanned the flames of a few latent fantasies all right.

"Why don't you have a seat? Can I get you something to drink?"

"Just water, thank you." He watched shapely calves and the gentle sway of her hips as she went to an armchair and sat down. A seat for one, he noticed. Not on the sofa where he might have sat beside her.

He got a glass from a cupboard and added crushed ice and water from the fridge dispenser. When he handed it to her, he noticed her hand was shaking. Whatever she wanted to tell him, she was nervous. Afraid.

And it hit him upside the head. The difference in her appearance. The first name only, the disappearing in the morning. It was all too cliché for it to be the first time she'd done this. God, was she here to tell him he needed to be tested for something? Go get antibiotics? He told himself to relax. They'd used protection after all.

He sat across from her and decided to just ask rather than dance around the topic. "Look, do I need to be tested for an STD or something? Is that why you're here?"

Her eyes widened and she choked on the water, coughing uncontrollably and he reached out, calmly removed the glass from her hand, and waited for the paroxysms to stop. When they finally did, her eyes had watered and there was an angry set to her lips.

"What the hell would give you that idea?"

"I don't know!" This whole situation was strange and surreal. "Hey, you're the one who disappeared before I got up and only gave me your first name. Now you show up weeks later, looking completely different and say you need to talk to me. If it's not an STD, what the hell..."

His mouth dropped open.

Her gaze slid to the floor.

"No," he whispered harshly. "No, it isn't possible. We used condoms."

She looked up, misery etched in every feature. "I assure you it is possible," she replied, reaching into her purse and withdrawing the positive test as proof. "I'm pregnant, and the baby's yours."

Chapter Two

His reaction was exactly what she'd expected, so why was she so disappointed?

"I was just as surprised as you," she murmured, twisting her fingers together as she looked up into his face. "This was so not in my plans right now."

"Or mine."

It would help if he didn't look so perfectly devastated. She had a sudden horrible thought. "God, you're not married, are you?"

He did laugh a little then, a huff of laughter that wasn't completely amused, but clearly the idea of being married was ridiculous. "No, not married. You can relax about that." He frowned. "And if I were, I wouldn't be cruising bars looking for some action."

Heat rose to her cheeks. "I didn't mean to insinuate…"

Chris sighed heavily. "Look, let's just cut to the chase. We're both single. We hooked up one night and something went wrong. Is that accurate? Assuming *you're* not married, of course. Or using me to be your baby daddy."

"What?" She leapt up, putting her hands on her hips. "Of course I'm not! What a joke!"

His expression darkened further. "So now I'm a joke?"

Lizzie took a deep breath and closed her eyes. "This is going all wrong." She gathered her thoughts and tried again. "Why don't we start at the beginning," she suggested. "Hi, I'm Lizzie Baron." She held out her hand.

"Lizzie Baron?" Now Chris stood up and stared at her as though she'd grown an extra head. "Like the Baron Energies Barons?"

She nodded, dropping the hand that he'd never shaken.

"Like Jacob and Jet's sister?"

She nodded.

"Which is why you were at the rodeo."

She nodded again. "I try to support my family, especially during local events."

"Drinking alone is a funny way to show your support."

Her lips twisted. Christopher Miller was a little too astute for her liking. She and her brothers didn't always see eye to eye. Jacob wanted to take on a bigger role at Baron, and she even agreed with him. But Brock had other ideas. Jacob kept putting pressure on her to help his cause but it wasn't that easy. Changing her father's mind was impossible once he'd made it up.

That particular weekend Jacob had nagged at her again and she'd gone to the bar to blow off some steam rather than argue. Chris had been there, all long legs and dark hair and rugged smiles. The perfect distraction.

"A girl can't go get a beer once in a while?"

He smiled then. "True enough." The smile faded. "You're really one of the Barons? And you're pregnant?"

"I'm afraid so. On both counts." She sighed. "Can we sit down again?"

"Sure." He gestured with his hand and she sat, then he followed suit. Manners, she realized, and was slightly encouraged.

Lizzie reached for her water again and took a sip, buying time to put her thoughts back together. "You deserved to hear it first," she said quietly. "Before I tell anyone else. I don't expect anything from you, Christopher, that's not why I came. I'm fully capable of supporting this baby on my own. This mistake doesn't have to be a big deal for you, okay? I certainly don't need child support or anything."

He raised one eyebrow. "I suppose you want me to sign away parental rights, too? No sign or trace of the rodeo bum, no stain on the great Baron name, right?"

Again her cheeks heated. "I didn't mean that at all! I just meant to say that I'm not here to… God, how do I put this? I'm not after anything from you. That's all. I'm handling it."

"Handling it." Chris put his hands on his knees and angled her a sharp look. "Does that mean you're *taking care of it?* Or am I reading that wrong?"

Taking care of it. She knew exactly what he meant. He was asking if she was going to terminate the pregnancy. "And would you care if I did?"

She was holding her breath as she waited for his answer. He met her gaze evenly.

"I would care," he finally said softly. "I've never really thought about it before, but it's not easy, is it? Theoretically I understand the right to choose. But when I think about this baby being part of me…" His gaze dropped to her stomach and back up. "I find I care very much, Lizzie."

It might have been easier if he didn't. If he were a bit more of a jerk, to be honest. Instead, even in his shock, he was remarkably level.

"Maybe you don't *need* help," he continued, "but it's here for you regardless. I always own up to my responsibilities."

Something warm slid through her at his gentle and

very unexpected words. "How can you say that when you've just found out? We hardly know each other. I mean, it took me a couple of days to even wrap my mind around the idea of this. I'm still reeling."

"There are some things you just know," he said calmly. "And then you figure the rest out as you go along."

She rested her palm on her tummy. Perhaps the most surprising thing of all was how protective she already felt towards her unborn child. The pregnancy was going to cause massive problems in both her professional and personal life. And yet there was something incredible about knowing that a tiny person resided inside her. It was frightening and it was awesome at the same time. In that moment, she forgot all about Baron Energies and Christopher Miller and anything else. Nothing was more important than this baby and making the right choices.

Her baby. She was no longer simply Lizzie Baron.

She was a mom.

It scared her to death.

There was a strange buzzing sound in the silence, followed by a series of chimes coming from the area around Lizzie's feet. She suddenly realized it was her cell, and the ringtone was the one she used for family, not work. "Excuse me just a moment," she said, reaching down and searching blindly in her bag.

The caller ID showed her stepmother Julieta's name, so she clicked the answer button. It only took a few short sentences for the blood to drain from her face.

"I'm glad I reached you," Julieta said, and Lizzie heard strain in her voice. "It's your dad, Lizzie. He got thrown and he's hurt."

Oh, hell. Brock Baron had always thought himself a bit indestructible, and persisted in competing in seniors' rodeos even though he was getting older. Lizzie closed her eyes and pinched the bridge of her nose. "How bad is it?"

"A badly broken leg, maybe a concussion, and they're checking his ribs for breaks, but he hasn't regained consciousness yet. Stupid, stupid man!"

Lizzie could hear the worry in Julieta's voice and she clutched the phone tightly, pressing it against her ear. "I'm not in Dallas at the moment," she said, and she heard the wobble in her voice, too. Damn it. Now was not the time to fall apart. Not that there was ever a good time. Her mind started to spin out of control as the ramifications of the call sank in, and she forced herself to deal with the crisis of the moment and not what lay ahead. "I can be there in a few hours, though. What about the rest of the family?"

"The boys are here, Savannah's coming right from the ranch, and Carly's on her way."

"Good, then you're not alone. I'll call you when I'm close, okay? And give him my love. Hang in there, Julieta."

She hung up the phone, dropped it in her bag and faced Chris again. "I'm sorry to cut this short. I know we have things to talk about, but I have to get back to Dallas right away."

His brows pulled together in concern. "Is everything okay?"

"Not really." Her voice wobbled and she cleared her throat. "My dad was in an accident. Far as we can tell, he's got a broken leg, but he's still unconscious and they're thinking he also has a concussion."

"Oh, my God. What happened?"

She shook her head, still not quite believing how full of himself her dad could be from time to time. His age and he still thought he was invincible. "He was competing. The events kicked off this morning. First round and he got thrown."

They both knew what could happen in the arena. "Of course you have to go. I understand."

She handed over a card from her wallet. "This is me, at Baron Energies. You can contact me there, okay? I don't want to tell the family about the baby yet. Especially now, when my dad…"

Her voice broke. Brock Baron was a crusty old bugger but he was her daddy and she still idolized him, faults and all. She stood up and suddenly her head felt light.

"Hey, Eliz…Lizzie, are you okay? You're white as a sheet."

She nodded and mustered up a smile. "I forgot to eat lunch is all, and got a bit light-headed." Which was a complete lie—she'd thrown up her breakfast and then by noon had been ravenous, wolfing down a bacon cheeseburger like a linebacker. Something about the red meat particularly appealed right now. But that was hours ago.

"I don't think you should be driving all that way by yourself. You're upset. Let me drive you."

She clutched the handle of her bag. "And throw you into the mix with my family? Not a chance."

"You can argue with me and waste time or you can say 'yes, Christopher' in that formal voice of yours and we can be on the highway in five minutes."

"I'm fine."

He raised an eyebrow.

Who knew the man could be so stubborn? "You can't order me around." She reached in the bag and found her keys, looping them around her finger. "And don't even try forcing my hand by bringing this secret into it."

Chris went up to her then, close enough she could see the little gold flecks in his rich brown eyes. Close enough she could smell his aftershave and close enough she could reach out and touch his strong chest if she wanted to.

Which she didn't. But if she did…

"Of course I'll do no such thing. But I will appeal to your common sense. I want you to be safe. The last thing your family needs is more bad news because you drove too fast or were distracted."

She was plenty distracted at the moment. Currently she was staring at his lips and remembering one glorious night in a discount motel room…

"If we take my car, how will you get back here?"

"I'll take the bus. Seriously, it's not that big a deal. I don't have any competitions this weekend. I was just going to go out to my folks' place and I can call and tell them I'll be a day or so late."

He put his hand along the side of her face, making the skin there tingle. "You're pale," he said softly. "And considering the news you shared with me today…"

"You should be running in the other direction."

"No, I shouldn't. Let me make sure you get to the hospital in one piece, okay? Besides, it gives us a chance to talk about all the things we need to on the way."

That actually made sense. Plus it would keep her mind off Brock and give her company for the drive—even if it was Chris.

"Okay. Can we get going though? I don't want to waste more time arguing."

He smiled then, and her heart gave a strange thump at the sight. It was the first time he'd truly smiled since she'd arrived, she realized. And she remembered why she'd fallen under his spell in the first place. Chris Miller was more than just handsome. He was…magnetic. She'd have to be careful to keep things totally platonic. There could be no romantic complications as they moved forward with her plans for the baby.

"We'll take my car. If I remember right, it's more comfortable than your truck."

"Deal." He put out his hand for the keys.

Reluctantly she gave them to him, and followed him out the door. They went down the elevator and through the foyer and out into the bright Texas sun, which seemed exceptionally warm for March. She squinted and pointed toward her car, but Chris just pushed the unlock button and found her vehicle when the lights flashed on.

"A Mercedes. Nice ride."

"It's a company car."

Which was strictly true. One of the perks of being a VP. Not that she was complaining…

He got behind the wheel and adjusted the mirrors and before she could exhale a deep breath he was pulling out of the parking lot. They were on their way to the highway when he pulled into a strip mall and zoomed into a drive-through. "What are you doing?"

"You looked like you were going to pass out back there. Let's get you something to eat, okay? You can eat while I drive."

She should protest, say they were wasting time, but the truth was she was hungry and she knew from bitter experience the last week or so that if she let herself get too famished, she got ill. "Just a roast beef sandwich and a milk for me, please."

He pulled up to the window and ordered two sandwiches, a milk and a Coke. She took out a twenty to pay for the meal, but he gave her a long stare and levered his hip, reaching for his wallet in his back pocket. "I think I can buy my kid a sandwich," he said quietly, taking out a couple of bills and handing them to the teenager at the window in exchange for the food.

She put her money away. So the man had his pride after all.

He didn't waste any time getting to the highway, headed toward Dallas and her family. It was strange seeing someone else in the driver's seat of her car, and surreal to think that he was the father of the baby growing inside her. None of it felt like it was truly possible; rather the situation was like a weird dream and she'd wake up with a great sense of relief. But it wasn't. She'd made a mistake. And now she had to deal with it, the way she'd always dealt with changing situations in her life. With logic.

The sandwich was delicious, a bit warm with tangy mustard and lettuce and tomato and she ate neatly, self-conscious the whole time. While she drank from her carton of milk, Chris manhandled his sandwich with one hand while driving and when the first half was gone, he reached for his soda and took a long pull. "Feel better?" he asked, looking over at her.

"I do, thank you." She tried a smile. She hadn't realized how hungry she was until she started eating. "You were right. I needed some fuel. Especially since I don't know when I'll eat again once I get to the hospital."

"You're close with your family?" He glanced over at her and then back at the road again.

"Mostly." It was a complicated question. "My mom left when we were pretty small—me and Savannah and Carly and Jet. When my dad remarried, he adopted Peggy's boys, Jacob and Daniel. Then Peggy died.... I think we're the new 'typical' American family." She smiled. "Blended a couple of times. Dad's current wife has a five-year-old son from a previous relationship. We get along pretty well—considering. Even though we've all grown, things are still centered out at the ranch. We've got the farm and Dad built the ring for rodeo training."

Chris nodded. "I don't come from a big family like that. Only child."

"Trouble sharing?" She grinned at him and he laughed a little.

"Not so much. Just a bit of pressure is all. All the expectations on the shoulders of one kid, you know?"

"That's not necessarily untrue in a big family. I've always felt like more was expected of me because I'm oldest. Even though Jacob and Daniel are pretty close to me in age, there was a difference as we grew up." She didn't say that it was partly because Brock treated the adopted boys just a little differently. She couldn't prove it, after all. And yet she was sure the boys sensed it just the same.

She put her head back against the seat rest. "Anyway, you know quite a bit about me now. How about you?"

His fingers gripped the wheel. "Not much to say, really. I grew up outside the city, had a pretty normal childhood. My dad was foreman on a ranch and the owner got me into rodeo."

"I saw that you were a junior champ a long time ago, but then it's like you dropped off the earth. Where've you been in the meantime? With rodeo being big in our family, I'm sure I would have heard your name before."

She wasn't sure why or if she'd touched a nerve, but Chris's jaw tightened. "I quit for a while."

"Injury?" Curious, she studied his profile.

"Obligations," he responded cryptically.

She let that sit for a few minutes, wondering if he'd expand on that terse statement. When he didn't, she asked. "What sort of obligations?"

"Does it matter?"

She nodded. "If I'm keeping this baby, and you're determined to do your duty, then we're going to be tied to each other for a very long time. I'd like to know what sort of guy is going to be my child's father, that's all."

His jaw ticked, but after a few moments he relented. "Look, my parents scrimped and saved to put me through university. No one else in my family had ever gone past high school. I took engineering at A&M and I've been working ever since. Until this year, I was an engineer at AB Windpower."

"Really? That's cool. I don't know a lot about them, but I've seen some write-ups about some of their energy initiatives. It's neat stuff. So why'd you leave?"

"This year is just a leave of absence."

"Why?"

"Why what?"

"Why the leave of absence?" She turned in the seat a little, tucking her left foot under her right leg and adjusting the seat belt on her shoulder.

"I missed competing," he said simply. "I've been working long hours for years now, cooped up inside for the most part. I wanted one year. Just one, to do what *I* wanted to do. To have some fun. So I asked my boss for a leave and I got it."

"You don't like being an engineer?"

"It's not that. Or at least… Hell, it's complicated."

Lizzie wasn't sure what to think about that. She had one brother who seemed allergic to responsibility and there were lots of times she'd had the thought that he needed to grow up. For some reason it had been easier to accept that Chris was a bronc rider when she didn't know he had a perfectly good, respectable career that he'd abandoned for a "year of fun." Then there was the

fact that she, apparently, was part of that year of irre-
sponsibility.

"It's always complicated," she responded, feeling the
comment was a bit useless but not knowing what else
to say.

The resulting silence was awkward. Lizzie had
thought company for the drive would be good, but hadn't
thought about how awkward it could be being shut up in
a car for hours with no escape. Thankfully it was only a
few minutes and Lizzie's phone rang again. Rather than
put it through the Bluetooth, she took it from her purse
and answered it. She'd rather not have family business
on speaker.

"Lizzie, it's Julieta. I wanted to give you an update."

Lizzie's stomach tightened nervously. "Is he okay?"

"Your father's just gone into surgery for his leg. The
concussion seems minor, no bleeding or anything so they
decided to go ahead."

"I'm getting there as fast as I can."

"Just get here safely. He'll be in surgery for a few hours
yet."

"Thanks."

"Ask at the desk at Emergency and they should be able
to tell you where we are, okay?"

"Sounds good." Lizzie hesitated and then felt the need
to ask. "Does anyone need anything?"

Julieta's voice was warm over the line. "We're fine.
You don't need to look after us, Lizzie. Now drive safe
and we'll see you soon."

Lizzie hung up, knowing she'd had the perfect opportunity to say she wasn't alone but for some reason hadn't.
She didn't want Chris to be a dirty little secret, but in her
mind he was. She was going to have to get over that. Her

family was going to find out sometime. Hiding Chris in a closet wasn't going to help anything.

"Anything wrong?" Chris asked, his voice concerned.

"They've taken my father into surgery." She frowned. "I know Julieta didn't say it, but he's not a spring chicken anymore. I'm worried about how hard this is going to be on his body."

"From everything I've heard, he's in great shape. I'm sure he'll be fine." Chris smiled encouragingly.

"I hope you're right," she said, sighing and leaning her head against the window.

He reached over and patted her leg, once, twice, and then put his hand back on the wheel.

But the gesture had given her more comfort than she'd expected, and when she closed her eyes she could see him standing before her in his apartment, claiming that he was going to take responsibility for their child. And as her breathing deepened, she pictured him as he'd been not even two months ago, his dark gaze boring into hers as they made love in the lamplight of the motel. The night her baby had been conceived…

CHRIS LOOKED OVER at Lizzie and frowned. She looked so peaceful now that she was sleeping, the lines of stress gone from her eyes and her lips slightly open as she took slow breaths.

Pregnant. Once he'd heard the word and absorbed the initial shock of the news, he'd done a pretty good job of holding it together. Of saying the right things. But that was nothing more than reaction in the very simplest terms. It was done and couldn't be changed. And it went without saying that he'd step up and do what was right. It was how he'd been raised.

But now that the reality was sinking in, he was freaking out a bit. A father! Sure, he'd have several months to get used to the idea, but it didn't alter the fact that his life was going to change. He was going to be tied to Lizzie Baron…forever.

A delicate snore came from the passenger seat and he looked over, unable to stop the wave of tenderness that washed over him. Maybe he was freaking out but he wasn't oblivious to the fact that she was facing the greatest changes right now. Heck, she'd turned a strange shade of whitish-green earlier and had needed to eat, and now she was sound asleep in the middle of the afternoon. He'd been right to drive her back to Dallas.

One night. One single night he hadn't been able to resist the temptation of her. One night when careful hadn't been careful enough…and now he could see his one year of freedom slipping further and further away.

She was beautiful. She'd been fair with him today and she was going to be the mother of his child. What a thing to have to wrap his head around.

But as he thought about his plans and how they'd suddenly been rendered irrelevant, he couldn't help but resent her just a little bit.

Chapter Three

Lizzie opened her eyes, instinctively putting her hand to the muscles in her neck that had tightened from the awkward angle in which she'd slept. A quick check showed they were nearly at the city limits. It wouldn't be long now and they'd be at the hospital. Good heavens, how long had she slept?

"Feel better?"

Chris's voice came from beside her and she turned her attention away from the view out the window. "I do. I didn't realize how tired I was."

"You probably work pretty long hours."

She snorted a little. Pretty long? Twelve-hour days were the norm. Her heart caught a little. What would happen now if her dad couldn't resume his place at Baron? There's no way she wanted Mark Baker at the helm. He was younger and a real go-getter, but he was also a part of that boys' club that made her feel as if she was going to get a pat on the head rather than the respect she'd earned. Especially since he seemed to hold a bit of a grudge where she was concerned.

Baron Energies should have a Baron at the head of the table. And the only Baron on the board right now was her.

And she was pregnant.

What a mess.

"My hours are probably about to get longer, with Dad away from the office for a while. Hopefully it'll just be a few weeks."

Hopefully.

"So when are you planning on telling them?"

Right, there was that, too. "I want my dad to let me run Baron while he's out of the office. If I tell him I'm pregnant...there's no way he'll agree." She sighed, looked over at Chris and wondered if they were becoming friends now, what with all this confiding. It seemed ludicrous. "This will be the first grandchild. I'm the oldest. He's a bit old school. I'll be fighting him tooth and nail even if I stay in my current position."

"So not for a while, then."

"Are you kidding? Add to that the fact that I'm single, and it's going to be one stressful conversation."

Single. Because they had had a one-night stand, not a relationship.

Could things be in a bigger mess?

"Is there anything I can do to help?"

She laughed a little. "Rewind eight weeks and not walk into the bar?"

And then she felt instantly sorry she'd said it. That wasn't fair. She'd been as willing a participant as he had. "Sorry," she murmured, looking away. "You're not to blame."

"Clearly I'm half to blame," he returned, slowing down to take an exit, but she could sense he was annoyed.

"You said you're going to take a bus back to San Antonio?"

"It makes the most sense."

"Maybe one of the boys can run you to the station."

"Wouldn't that require an explanation?"

Damn it. And yet asking him to walk or take public transit seemed cold. Like she was…ashamed. Determined to keep him out of sight, and that didn't sit well with her. She wasn't brought up to sneak around. Besides, he'd given up hours of his day to drive her here when he didn't have to.

Traffic slowed as they neared the city center and Lizzie tapped her fingers on her knee. At some point her family would meet Chris. Heck, Jacob and Jet already knew him, at least a little. What if he came inside rather than being pushed aside, invisible? She had a sudden flash of inspiration. What if Lizzie could bring the family around to this gradually, so it wasn't such a shock?

"I was thinking…rather than disappear to the station, maybe you'd like to come in? Just because we show up together doesn't mean we have to tell my family everything, does it?"

He stopped at a traffic light and looked over at her, his dark eyes piercing. "You're scheming, aren't you?"

She tried a small smile. "Not scheming, planning. Planning is what I do best. I get fewer surprises that way."

Lizzie wasn't a fan of surprises. Several had come her way over the years that she couldn't control, but she tried to keep them to a minimum in her own life. Now that she was pregnant, she realized she hadn't done such a stellar job.

"What if I introduce you and just, I don't know, say that we were together when I got the call and you offered to drive?"

"Together? In San Antonio?"

She bit down on her lip. "Oh. Right. Well, we could always say that we've been seeing each other a little, but we weren't saying anything because it was early days."

"You mean lie."

"It's not technically a lie. We have seen each other a little…"

"It's deliberately misleading them, so yeah, in my books that's a lie."

The light changed and he moved through the intersection. On one hand, his stubborn stance annoyed her but on the other, she admired his honesty. "So what, you just want to walk in and say 'hey, I'm Chris, and I knocked up Lizzie?'"

Now it was his turn to look perturbed. "I didn't say that."

"So what if they think we've been seeing each other? It'll make breaking the news easier."

"What you mean is it'll make it look better, right? I mean, getting accidentally pregnant by your boyfriend looks marginally better than picking up some guy in a bar."

"You don't have to make it sound so crude." Yes, they'd hooked up. But it hadn't been… Lizzie swallowed thickly. That night it had seemed as though they'd known each other forever. He hadn't felt like a stranger. Perhaps that's why she'd truly let go with him. As much as she didn't want to admit it, being beside him now caused the same sort of stirrings she'd felt that night. She wasn't as immune as she'd like to pretend.

Chris pulled into the hospital parking lot. "Sorry. It wasn't crude." He slid the car into a vacant space and looked over at her. "It was awesome."

And just like that the air in the car seemed to get heavier. Full of promise and caution all at the same time.

His gaze held hers for far too long as the engine idled. In the space of those moments, Lizzie recalled so many things about that night. The way he smiled, the warmth in his eyes, replaced by a heat so scorching she thought she might be singed by it as his hands touched her body. The sound of his voice in the dark, the low, rich chuckle in the shadows. How he'd opened his arms and let her curl up against him rather than looking for an escape route.

Chris Miller was no more the bad guy here than she was. And because of it she was compelled to agree with him. "You're right," she answered shyly. "It was awesome."

Silence filled the car once more.

"Look," she said quietly. "I'm not ready to come right out and tell everyone the news, especially now. I want to wait for the dust to settle. But I don't want to treat you like some dirty little secret, either. I went to find you today to start us talking. To give us a chance to make some decisions before having to deal with my family. The Barons aren't exactly…subtle."

She undid her seat belt and turned in the seat until she was facing him completely. "Chris, when I go in there they're going to ask questions anyway, about what I was doing over three hours away from Dallas on a workday. If I say I was taking care of some personal business they won't let it drop. I was willing to face that before, but now I'm thinking…if we went in there together, maybe it wouldn't be so bad for them to come to their own conclusions. It could buy us some time to figure this all out. Plus…"

Her voice faltered and she looked down at her hands. Her nails were precisely painted and beautifully manicured. Where had the outdoor-loving, ranch-riding girl gone? She was lost behind a power suit and a pair of heels.

"Plus what, Lizzie?"

She looked up again. "Plus it might be nice to not have

to walk in there alone. I know Dad's going to be okay, but I hate hospitals. Have ever since I was a little girl."

Ever since her mother had been there when Jet was born. When Delia had come home, she hadn't been the same mom who'd gone in to have her fourth baby. Lizzie had never forgotten that, and remembering it now made her grossly uncomfortable. She was about to become a mother, too. She was only a few weeks along and she couldn't imagine ever abandoning her child the way her mother had abandoned them.

"Are you asking me to be your wingman?" He turned off the car and rested his hand on the steering wheel.

She turned her attention back to him, gratefully. "Would you mind? Add it to the list of crazy stuff to happen to you today."

She was rewarded with another reluctant smile.

"Seriously, Chris. Then tomorrow we can worry about getting you back home."

He blew out a breath. "This is turning out to be the strangest day," he admitted, running a hand over his hair. "I'm still trying to come to grips with the fact that you're…you're having my baby."

"I know. This wasn't at all how I planned it would go."

"Everything is going to change and you want me to waltz into the hospital as if we're old pals."

"I'm sorry.…"

"Don't be sorry. You're probably right about there being fewer questions now rather than later when everyone isn't preoccupied."

"I'm sure everyone will be more focused on my dad than us anyway."

"Then let's go. Your family is probably wondering where you are."

Lizzie called Julieta's cell as they walked across the

parking lot and into the building. They stopped at information and got the details about Brock and then proceeded to the surgical floor, where the rest of the Barons were congregated. Lizzie hesitated for a moment, staring through the doors at the collection of people—Julieta and her son, Alex, Lizzie's younger sisters, Savannah and Carly, and then the boys—Jet and Jacob and Daniel. She pressed a hand to her stomach, suddenly afraid. She'd always tried to be the responsible one. How easy it would be for them to throw her mistake in her face once they found out how reckless she'd been.

Chris reached down and took her hand in his. It was warm and a bit rough and very, very comforting.

"You okay?"

She'd lived through their mother leaving. She'd lived through her stepmother dying and all the grief that had followed—for all of them. "I'll be fine," she replied. "Let's go."

But as they went through the door, she didn't let go of his hand.

Savannah saw her first. "Lizzie! You're finally here!" She came forward quickly, sparing Chris a curious glance before enveloping Lizzie in a hug.

"How is he?" Lizzie asked, stepping back. Savannah must have come right from the ranch store. She was still wearing her Peach Pit work shirt and jeans. "Any word?"

Julieta came forward, her normally perfect hairstyle slightly frayed around the edges, her eyes tired, and yet still incredibly beautiful. "He's just out of surgery," she said softly. "Still in recovery, so it'll be a while before we can see him."

"And everything went well?" Lizzie's insides clenched at the thought of her father, her dynamic, energetic, blustery father lying motionless on a surgical table.

"As far as we know." Julieta saw Chris standing just behind Lizzie and smiled at him. "Hello, I'm Julieta, Brock's wife." There was no mistaking the Spanish lilt to her voice.

Chris stepped forward and held out his hand. "Chris Miller, ma'am."

"Chris was with me when you called," Lizzie explained, her cheeks heating. "He drove me to the hospital."

"How nice of you," Julieta remarked, while Lizzie was aware of the rest of the family looking on.

"Long drive for someone who's worried about their family," he explained simply. "I was glad to do it."

"Miller? Chris Miller, is that you?"

Lizzie saw Jet stepping forward, his face registering surprise. Of course they would know each other. Rodeo was really a small world when all was said and done.

"Jet." Chris smiled again and held out his hand. "Good to see you. Sorry about your dad."

The men clasped hands firmly. "You and Lizzie?" Jet looked between the two of them. "Since when?"

Lizzie stepped in, not trusting Chris to answer. "Since about eight weeks ago." She could feel Chris's gaze on her face and she refused to look at him.

"Eight weeks?" Jet's lips dropped open. "Well, aren't you the one for keeping secrets, Miss I'll-Never-Date-A-Cowboy." He winked at her.

Her brother was far too astute and far too charming for his own good. "I have a family who tends to make everything their business," she said wryly. "Figured I'd better keep it under the Baron radar or else you'd tell him stories and scare him away. Besides, you're the last person qualified to give me a dating lecture." She raised an eyebrow at him. Jet never had any problem getting girls.

He attracted them like bees to honey with his good looks and easy charm. He was a bit like their father that way. "Chris came for moral support," she added.

She hoped God wasn't about to strike her down with a bolt of lightning, the way the lies were tripping off her tongue with such ease. And she totally ignored what Jet said about not dating cowboys. She wasn't exactly opposed to them, but if she didn't say she was, her family would be trying to set her up left and right.

Chris didn't say anything, to her great relief. But he did come closer and put his arm around her, resting his hand on her waist. The touch seared through her jacket to her skin.

For the next several minutes she caught up with Carly, who had also driven up from Houston, and her stepbrothers, Jacob and Daniel, who sat away from the rest of the family and chatted quietly, their elbows on their knees. Jacob and Daniel resembled each other heavily, from their dark hair and eyes to their body language. Chris knew Jacob from the circuit as well, and she was relieved because it eased the tension that always seemed to simmer just below the surface of the family. Julieta's son, Alex, had fallen asleep curled up in a chair, but when he woke up he was out of sorts. The doctor had just come to speak to them though, and the sound of his whining was disconcerting.

"Hey, Alex, are you hungry?" Chris stepped forward and squatted down in front of the boy. "I haven't had any dinner. How's about you and me go to the cafeteria and see what they've got to eat?"

Alex's brown eyes looked innocently into Chris's. "I can'ts go with you 'cause you're a stranger."

Lizzie's heart warmed as Chris smiled and looked to Julieta for backup.

Julieta excused herself for a moment and came to Alex's side. "This is Chris, Alex. He came with Lizzie, and he's okay. If you want to go to the cafeteria, you can. Maybe you can grab Mama something to eat, too, okay?"

"Can I have money?" he asked. "So I can pay all by myself?"

Lizzie tried not to smirk. The kid was learning early.

"Of course." Julieta took a few bills out of her purse and gave them to Chris. "Chris will look after them for you, okay? And if you aren't a good boy, he won't let you pay for the food." She gave him a stern look.

"Yes, Mama."

"Ready?" Chris asked.

Alex nodded and Chris stood. Lizzie watched them head for the unit doors and her heart gave a strange thump against her ribs as Alex reached up and trustingly put his small hand in Chris's.

The family turned their attention back to the doctor, who was explaining the procedure to put a rod in Brock's leg, the plan for the next few days and the concerns they had for his recovery. Lizzie was disheartened to hear that recuperation could take from four to six months, especially for a man of Brock's age. He was in general good health, which was in his favor, but with the added concussion, though minor, what he needed most right now was time and rest and once he was ready they'd start on rehab.

After he left, Julieta sat down, her face drawn, and Lizzie looked at Jet.

"Well, little brother, if you were ever going to reconsider going into the family business…"

Jet scowled. "I'm in the family business. Rodeo. On my own ranch, thanks."

"That's not what I meant and you know it." She kept her voice low, not wanting the whole family to overhear her putting the screws to her brother. "Dad's not going to be able to go into work for a while. You know he wants you as part of the business."

"And you're already a vice president. You're the one to take the reins now, sis."

She scoffed. "Right. Like the board is going to stand for that."

"It will if Dad says so."

"And will he? Because he'd rather it were you. I swear, if he puts Mark Baker in the driver's seat I'll resign. That man is impossible."

"You won't resign. You love that company as much as Dad does."

She sighed. He was right. So what was she going to do? Run an entire energy company in between bouts of morning sickness and prenatal appointments?

She squared her shoulders. Well, why not? If she didn't, she'd just prove every chauvinistic thing Mark Baker ever said absolutely true.

"You're sure you won't come aboard?"

Jet smiled his charming smile. "I'm sure you'll do a great job, Liz. And I'll tell Dad that, too, if it helps."

"Yeah, thanks a lot," she answered halfheartedly.

Jet disappeared after that, and she caught sight of him texting in a corner of the waiting room. She took a seat and slid off her heels, which were starting to hurt her feet. She leaned back and closed her eyes as exhaustion began to creep in. Maybe they'd soon be allowed to see Brock and then she could go home to her comfy apartment and bed....

"Lizzie?"

It was Jacob this time, looking incredibly earnest. She knew right away why he'd come to sit with her. While Jet couldn't be convinced to take on a bigger role at Baron Energies, Jacob wanted one and Brock kept holding out.

"Hey," she said tiredly.

"Looks like Dad's going to be out of commission for a while. Do you think that puts you in charge?"

"I don't know. Maybe."

"I'd be happy to step up, take on a bigger part at the company if that would help you out, ease some of the pressure."

Lizzie considered her words. Jacob was a good man and they tended to think a lot alike. She didn't understand why Brock kept him in the wings at Baron. She also knew that his offer came from a genuine willingness to help, and not really from trying to advance his personal position.

"I'll let you know. I appreciate the offer, Jacob, but I'm going to have to run everything by Dad, you know that. Even if he does have to hand day-to-day control over to someone…me…I can't sanction changes he wouldn't make. You understand that, right?"

"Shit would hit the fan," Jacob acknowledged with a smile. "I'm going to be on the road a lot this summer. The one thing I do that he seems to approve of is rodeo." He frowned. "But will you promise that if you need anything, you'll ask?"

"I will, but Jacob, it's not even a done deal."

"Sure it is. We all know who he'd like to have running the company…." Jacob looked over at Jet in the corner. "But he relies on you and you're family. That trumps everything."

"So are you," she pointed out. Sure, she remembered the time before Peggy and the boys had come on the scene, but they had been a part of their lives for so long

there was no question about their place in the family—
at least for her.

"In a way I'm glad I'm not you." He grinned suddenly.
"He's going to hate being at home and away from the office. I bet he calls you a dozen times a day."

The unit doors opened again and a grinning Alex
burst through, carrying a paper bag nearly as big as he
was, Chris following closely behind with a cardboard
tray of cups in one hand and a sack in the other.

The two ten-dollar bills Julieta had given Alex
wouldn't have come close to paying for the sheer volume of food they brought back, and she looked at Chris
with something that felt like affection. Damn it, she was
starting to like him on top of everything else.

That probably wouldn't be a good idea, would it? Especially if the goal was to keep things logical and businesslike. He stopped and handed her a hot cup. "I thought
you could use an herbal tea," he said quietly, so close to
her ear that shivers snuck deliciously down her spine.
"Sadly, the other sack is full of doughnuts and cinnamon
buns. You may have to make a sacrifice."

She took the cup and wrapped her hands around its
warmth. "It was nice, what you did," she said, looking up
and meeting his gaze. "It's a long day for Alex."

"He's a great kid," Chris replied. "A lot of energy,
but great." His smile was a little crooked. Lizzie found
it endearing.

"I don't know how long we're going to be here." Lizzie
took a restorative sip. "But you're welcome to stay at
my place for tonight. My couch is pretty comfortable."

"I appreciate it."

"Oh please. You totally dropped everything for me
today and under what might have been really tense circumstances. I appreciate it, Chris. I think it's a good sign,

really, for how we'll be able to deal with each other in the months ahead."

Right. Because they weren't actually dating. It was all an act for tonight. And the details to be worked out were more like a business negotiation than a relationship.

A nurse approached the group. "If you're waiting for Brock Baron, you can see him now. Just for a few minutes. Follow me."

Chris took her cup from her fingers. "Go," he ordered, nudging her forward. "I'll wait for you here."

She followed the nurse along with the rest of the family, suddenly nervous. She wasn't ready. Not ready to sit at the head of the boardroom table, and definitely not ready for motherhood—and she was, in all reality, being thrust into both roles at the same time.

Chapter Four

Chris rolled over and lifted an arm over his head, staring up at the ceiling of Lizzie's condo. It was coolly modern, decorated in a lot of black, white and chrome. Beautiful, he supposed, but a little sterile and missing out on the coziness he'd been expecting. It was decorated much like an executive suite rather than a home. The sofa had been comfortable enough though his feet dangled over the end, and she'd given him a soft comforter and nice pillow. And at first he'd slept okay.

But then he'd opened his eyes while it was still dark outside and he hadn't been able to get back to sleep.

Yesterday had been stupidly surreal and when he put all the pieces of what had happened together, it was hard to believe. He'd known Jet and Jacob for a while, and everyone was familiar with the Baron business, but he'd never crossed paths with Lizzie until that night in the bar.

She should seem more of a stranger to him, but there was a familiarity that was surprising. He sighed deeply. A logical man would be wondering about a paternity test. A cautious guy wouldn't take everything she said at face value. It wasn't like she'd been all that transparent at their first meeting....

And yet he did believe her. He couldn't explain why, especially when he tended to be a bit cynical at the best of times. Somehow it felt as though he'd known her longer. There was a comfort level that was unique. Under the circumstances, a guy would shy away from family drama like the Barons had gone through yesterday.

Instead he'd inserted himself right in the middle. And he'd enjoyed seeing Jet and Jacob, liked taking the innocent and impish Alex to the cafeteria.

He had yet to meet Brock, but the truth was he liked her family. It was big and complicated and caring—the sort of noisy, loving family he'd never had but always wanted, growing up as an only child.

But there was still the matter of Lizzie, and the fact that she wasn't interested in him personally—she was only interested in how they were going to handle the logistics of parenthood. It was the strangest start to a relationship he'd ever had. Only six months ago Erica had bailed on him and he'd seen her true colors. She'd wanted what he could provide more than she wanted him. She'd wanted the paycheck, the house and the white-picket fence. And when he'd turned his back on his job to go rodeoing, she'd left, saying he wasn't the man she thought he was.

There was no danger of Lizzie wanting him for his stability and security. She had Baron money backing her up. He wasn't sure how he felt about that, either. The truth was she was having his kid and she didn't need him in any way. What would keep her from shutting him out of his child's life if things went badly?

He was still lost in his thoughts when he heard footsteps shuffling on the upper level of the condo, followed by the most pitiful sound of retching he'd ever heard.

Morning sickness. The perfect reminder that she was far more affected by this pregnancy than he was—at least for the moment.

It was rude to listen but he didn't see how it could be avoided. After a very long few minutes, the toilet flushed and he heard water running. He'd better get up and get moving.

He was dressed and in the process of folding up the comforter she'd given him when she came downstairs, freshly showered and dressed in neat trousers, low heels and a blousy pink top with asymmetric ruffles across the front. She looked quite pretty, he realized, except her eyes looked tired and her face still held a grayish-green pallor.

"Good morning." He felt completely out of his depth.

She tried to smile back, but it didn't quite make it. "I'd offer you coffee, but I don't have any in the house. I can't stand the smell of the stuff these days."

"That's okay." He finished folding the blanket and put it on the end of the sofa. Smells, too? Clearly he wasn't familiar with the ins and outs of pregnancy.

"Do you want some breakfast? I'm fairly well stocked. There's cereal or eggs or oatmeal. Bread for toast."

"What are you having?"

"Some buttered toast."

"That works for me. What can I do?"

She shrugged. "Nothing, really."

He went into the kitchen anyway and took the loaf of bread from her hands. He slid two pieces into the toaster. "Where's your butter and a knife?"

Wordlessly she got out two plates, a knife and two glasses. "Apple juice okay? I can't seem to handle the acid in the orange in the morning."

"Apple's fine," he answered, marveling at the peculiarities of pregnancy once more. He was so over his head and unsure of how to proceed. Never mind he still had to get back to his place so he could head to his mom and dad's. He hadn't wanted to give them much information last night when he'd called to say he wouldn't be arriving for a few days. Some news was better delivered in person—and after he and Lizzie had made a plan of some sort.

The toast popped and he buttered it, but as he was putting it on a plate Lizzie disappeared again, this time into the downstairs half bath. The slammed door didn't do much to muffle the sounds coming from within.

He ate the two pieces of toast that were prepared, not really noticing the taste. It was only a few minutes when Lizzie came back out, her smile a little easier now.

"I should be good now," she said hopefully. "I find I'm only really sick first thing in the morning. I guess I didn't get it all out the first time." She blushed a little and Chris thought she looked adorable. "Is there any more toast?"

"How can you think about eating?" He stared at her.

She laughed a bit. "Actually, it's normally better if I can eat a little first. The empty stomach is the worst for the nausea."

"Any other things I should be aware of?" he asked, plopping two more slices of bread into the slots.

Lizzie handed him a glass of juice. "Well, I get sleepy and tend to nap and not always at the best time. I've also had to start wearing less fitted clothing, because I'm not showing yet but my waist seems to be getting bigger all of a sudden."

Changes. So many of them.

"How'd things go with your dad last night?" He handed her the hot toast. Lizzie had barely spoken to him on the drive home, and then when they'd arrived she'd made sure he had bedding before she went up to her room. The dark circles were still slightly visible under her eyes. Without asking, he'd understood that seeing her dad in the hospital bed and the long day had taken a toll.

Lizzie perched on a bar stool and nibbled. "It was rough. He looked so gray, and he was awake but very groggy from the anesthetic and pain meds. He's usually up and giving orders, you know?"

"So what happens now?"

"I suppose I go back to the hospital today and see how he's doing, and then take you back to San Antonio."

"Don't you think we should talk about what we're going to do?"

She took a bigger bite of toast, chewed, swallowed. It was almost as if the bite bought her time to think. To deliberate how to put her next words. "Well, I don't actually need you to 'do' anything. It's not like we're…well…"

Her gaze met his and his pulse jumped again. He frowned. The problem was he kept having these reactions to her and he didn't want to. It muddied the waters too much. Plus there was the baby to think about. They needed to set the boundaries of their relationship now so there was no confusion later. "How do you see me participating?" He finished his toast and put his plate in the sink.

"I don't know, to be honest," she replied. "Financially I'm okay. I guess I was just thinking you needed to know and not much beyond that."

That she didn't need his money was a slight relief but it also didn't sit well. What kind of man would he be if he didn't help support his own kid? Certainly not the man his father raised. And his mom and dad were already perplexed about his choice to leave the company for a year to pursue rodeo. *A waste of time,* they'd called it. *Impractical.*

He set his teeth. Why did it always come down to

doing the things that other people wanted him to do rather than what he wanted?

Erica's parting words echoed in his ears. *"You're not who I thought you were,"* she'd accused. *"I thought you were stable, reliable, going somewhere. And all you can think about is playing with your damned horses."*

The one time he made a choice for himself and look what happened. There was no way he could "play" at rodeo for the whole season when there was a baby on the way. There were medical bills to pay. Things that Lizzie would need. And he had enough pride to be determined that she wouldn't shoulder all that herself. Yeah, he'd taken the year off after calculating he had enough to cover his own expenses. But this was definitely an extra he hadn't counted on.

Then there was Lizzie herself. It bugged him that she expected so little. And it bugged him that she seemed so completely immune to him. It wasn't so long ago that she'd been in his arms, surrendering to his touch. He swallowed heavily and tried to banish the image that fired through his brain.

"The truth is, I don't know what the hell I want," he answered honestly. "I think we both need time to think about it, sort things through. I'm having a hard time thinking of myself as a dad. And we barely know each other."

Maybe, but it was hard not to get lost in the deep blue of her eyes. They were large and thickly lashed and stood out especially with her hair pulled back away from her face. He couldn't be faulted for his attraction, could he? She was a beautiful woman.

"I'm struggling with that, too," she admitted. "I always thought I'd start with my career at Baron, and then fall in love and get married and then think about kids."

"All on a well-executed schedule?"

"Something like that." She smiled weakly at him.

"I always thought I'd work with horses," he admitted. "I loved rodeo and still do, but more than that I loved working in the barns, taking care of the stock, just like my dad. I used to help him at the ranch where he worked. Followed him around like a devoted puppy." He grinned.

"What happened?"

Chris shrugged. "My parents wanted more for me. I showed a good head for numbers and liked science. I mostly took engineering to please them. They worked hard to save enough to help send me to university. It felt like the right thing to do."

"You don't like it?"

"It's all right." He frowned. He always felt a little guilty about not being happier in his profession. "It's a good living. And I've been able to help them out from time to time, pay them back for my education."

She nodded. "That's too bad. That you're not happy, that is. My sister Savannah manages the store on the ranch, and she loves it. You can see it in her face when you walk in, she's smiles from ear to ear. I might not be quite that open with my feelings, but I always wanted to work with Dad at Baron."

"And you like Human Resources?"

"Sure. I like people. I like thinking about their personalities, strengths, weaknesses, how they interact with other people, seeing who'd make a good fit on a team. I think I get a good sense of things and it made me good at my job."

"Made?"

"I'm not quite as hands-on as I used to be. Most of that is left to my manager and his staff."

Chris nodded. "And now you're looking at having to step into the driver's seat."

She raised her eyebrows in a "what are you going to do?" look. "It appears so. I guess the one good thing about it is that Dad should be back before the baby's born."

He hadn't even thought to ask about a due date. A quick calculation in his mind put him at mid-October. "What is the official date, anyway?"

"October twelfth."

An autumn baby. His parents would be thrilled.

She checked her watch. "I suppose I should get to the hospital."

"I'll get ready," he suggested. "I don't want to hold you up."

She looked surprised. "I don't expect you to hang around there again, you know. Yesterday you went way above and beyond."

There she was, pushing him away again. "Wouldn't it be easier to go with you, and then we can leave right from the hospital instead of backtracking?"

"People will get the wrong idea."

He pursed his lips. "So what? Eventually they are going to know we had sex. You said it yourself. Showing up together makes it look like there was more to it than a one-nighter. Unless there's another reason why you don't want me around?"

She blushed.

"Is there another reason, Lizzie?"

"Like what?" She lifted her chin and he saw the spark of defiance in her eyes. He liked it. Liked her when she got a little fired up. She'd been this way before, too. A little on edge. Exciting.

He moved closer to her, saw her pupils widen and

that's when he knew. The cool, calm demeanor wasn't completely real. Oh, he had no doubt that she wanted it to be, but it wasn't. Another step put him directly in front of her, close enough he could smell the light floral scent of her shampoo, see the way her pulse beat heavily at her throat. Pounding the way his was pounding. The pull between them was still there, strong as ever.

"What are you doing?" she whispered.

"Shh," he ordered, as he contemplated his next move.

Chris touched his lips to hers, testing, and felt a familiar jolt rush through him, zinging from his fingers through to his toes. What was it about this woman that fired his passion so completely? Yesterday there'd been too much to take in, too much information to process, but today was different. Today was slower. Less of a shock. And to his surprise, the taste of her lips was achingly familiar even though he'd only tasted them once before.

She opened to him a little, shyly at first, and he put his hand along the small of her back and drew her closer. Her arms lifted around his neck and he deepened the kiss by degrees until his tongue touched hers and the flame flickering inside him threatened to ignite completely. Reluctantly he pulled back, leaving his hands on her hips as the kiss broke off.

"What the hell?" she whispered, a furious tone in her voice. "That is not part of the plan!"

"We don't even have a plan. Every time we go to talk about it, the subject changes."

"Well, excuse me." She wiped her hand across her lips. "I haven't exactly been in this position before."

"Well, neither have I! You're the one who likes to have everything organized and tied up with a ribbon, aren't you? And every time we get close to saying what we want, one of us backs away."

She pursed her lips.

"Do you want to raise him or her alone, then?" he persisted. "And me completely out of the picture?"

"I don't know!" She raised her voice, and he could see she was not in the calm control she longed for.

"That's right. You don't know. Neither do I. And this baby isn't coming for several months yet. Why do we need to decide right now?"

"Because I…because…" She floundered, running a hand over her neat hair. "Because we should start as we mean to go on."

"Says who? We barely know each other. Maybe we should work on that before making written-in-stone decisions."

"I don't see how kissing me fits into a…a custodial arrangement."

"Lizzie," he said quietly. "There was something between us because otherwise we wouldn't have made this baby. If there's still something between us, we should address it, don't you think?"

Her gaze slid away. "I can't think about this right now. My dad's in the hospital. I'm going to have to manage the company while he's out and I have to focus on that."

"That and taking care of yourself," he reminded her.

"Well, of course that!" She backed away from him. "You're just mixing me up, Chris."

He'd been thinking how he was dealing with an overload of information, but now he realized that Lizzie was dealing with even more. Her emotions were being pulled in several directions. Maybe she could only handle one thing at a time.

In which case she was right. Kissing her hadn't been fair, even though it had been very enlightening. The spark was still there.

"Let's go then, and leave the rest for another time."

Her face softened with a sliver of gratitude and she reached for her purse and briefcase.

No one seemed surprised to see Chris with Lizzie at the hospital waiting room. Savannah had come in early before opening the store for the Saturday crowd, and Carly had gone for coffee for everyone. Julieta and Alex were there already, Alex looking bored as he listlessly colored in a coloring book. The boys had gone off to wherever, not competing this weekend but not at the hospital either.

Lizzie smiled at her family but it was Alex who responded with enthusiasm.

"Chris!" He got up out of his chair, scattering crayons, and ran to Chris's side, looking up expectantly. "Can we go ride the elevator?"

Chris laughed and Lizzie absorbed the sound, so easy and, well, *manly*. Only minutes ago he'd been standing in her kitchen kissing her. Kissing!

So much for keeping this strictly business. And the worst part of it was, she'd liked it. Too much.

"Hey, squirt. Hang on a few minutes, okay?" He smiled down at Alex and looked at Julieta. "Hospital's not much of a fun place for a boy, huh."

Julieta's eyes were troubled. "During the week he has school and then after-school care, and our housekeeper is always around. Usually the weekends aren't an issue. Except…"

"Of course, you need to be here."

Savannah came down the hall and into the waiting area. Lizzie was always a little envious of her sister. Her dark hair fell in a smooth bob and she had skin that Lizzie hadn't seen since she was twelve. Even in her casual work-wear of jeans and a store T-shirt, Savannah had a natural beauty that shone.

"Oh, hey, Chris." Savannah smiled and then looked to Julieta and Lizzie. "He's awake and grouchy."

Lizzie laughed, relieved. "In other words, he's feeling his old self."

"Yeah. Of course, my peaches and cream muffins helped soften him up a little. I've got to get back to open the store but I'll come in after we close for the day, okay?"

"Of course." Lizzie smiled at her. Savannah had such a nurturing streak, and had channeled that into a very successful business, running the ranch store where she sold their produce as well as all sorts of jams, jellies and baked goods. The one bone of contention seemed to be Brock, who insisted on maintaining ownership rather than handing off that whole side of the business to Savannah. "He'll need to rest some anyway," Lizzie assured her sister. "Don't worry."

Lizzie gave her sister a hug and watched as she walked down the white-tiled hall, stopping to talk to Carly for a moment as the younger sister brought back two cups of coffee and a bottle of juice for Alex.

Lizzie turned and saw Chris watching her curiously. *Kissing her in the kitchen...*

Carly's voice chided her. "I didn't know you were coming so early. I didn't get you coffee."

"That's okay. I don't need it anyway." She tried a smile, grateful to not be in the position to have to refuse. "Who's next up? Do you mind if I sneak in to see Dad now? I'm driving Chris back to San Antonio and want to get an early start."

"Sure, go ahead." Carly nodded. "I could stand some caffeine before going a few rounds with him." She of-

fered a wry smile, and Lizzie reached back and gave
Carly's thick braid a tug.

"You are not to deliberately provoke him, okay?"

Carly grinned. "Most of the time I can't help it." But
then Carly's smile softened. "Don't worry, Lizzie. He's
a stubborn pain in the neck but we're all just thankful
he's okay. No arguments. I promise."

Lizzie gripped her purse tighter, hoping that Brock
was in his gruff but amenable mood this morning. Or that
the painkillers were working. Beside her, Chris spoke
to Alex. "Hey, partner, have you checked out the gift
shop yet?"

Alex shook his head soberly.

"You want to?"

To his credit, Alex looked to his mother for permission. "Go ahead," she said. "Chris—thanks. I know he's
a handful."

"He's a boy, that's all. I'll see if I can find out what
Brock's favorite junk food is and sneak in some con-
traband."

Alex piped up right away. "He likes chips and beer."

Lizzie choked out a laugh as Chris and Alex walked
away, Chris explaining that beer might be a tough thing
to get hold of in a hospital.

"He seems like a good guy, Lizzie. I'm happy for you."
Julieta's voice was quiet by her side. Carly sat in a chair
flipping through a magazine.

"It's… Yeah." Lizzie hesitated, not sure how to explain
their relationship at all and yet hating lying about it. "I'd
better get in there. If I'm not out in fifteen minutes, send
Rangers in the direction of the shouting."

"You're going to talk work, aren't you?" Julieta's calm
face switched to an expression of disapproval.

"Only as much as I have to. Enough so I know what's

going on when I walk into the office on Monday morning."

"Go easy. He doesn't need the stress."

Neither do I, Lizzie thought, shouldering her bag and heading to the hospital room.

Brock was lying in the bed, a blue blanket covering him to his hips, still dressed in a hospital gown. His color was paler than usual, his gray hair limp on his head. There was a newspaper on his lap, but it was abandoned and his eyes were closed.

She turned around to leave when his voice stopped her. "I'm awake. No need to run away with your tail between your legs."

Stay calm, she reminded herself, *and don't let him provoke you.* Pushing a person's buttons and then gauging their reaction was a Brock Baron litmus test. One she'd become pretty adept at passing.

"How're you feeling?" she asked, perching on the bed.

"Like I got run over by a bull. Oh wait. I did."

"Yes, you did, you big fool. What on earth were you doing bull riding anyway?"

"It was a seniors' rodeo and I'm not in my grave yet."

"You're going to be if you keep up this foolishness."

He lifted an eyebrow as his eyes cleared. "You're starting to sound like my wife and not my daughter."

"That's probably because we both love you, you old coot."

His face softened then. "Hard to argue against that now, isn't it? Glad you're giving me a hard time like normal. All the long looks around here and I was starting to worry I wouldn't be okay."

She sighed and relaxed. "I'm under firm orders not to upset you. But really—how are you?"

"The pain's okay. Head hurts a bit, which is why the

lights are low. The painkillers are taking care of most of it."

"Good."

"Doc said it's going to be a long haul, but I'll be up and around before you know it. You wait and see."

This was where it was going to be difficult. "Dad, it's going to be a little while at least. I can step in at the office until you're back to full strength."

"I was thinking Jet should step in. Perfect time for him to take on more responsibility."

This was what she'd been afraid of. "Dad," she said gently, "I know you want Jet to be part of the business but he's simply not interested. I talked to him about it last night...."

"And talked him out of it?"

She heard the accusation in his voice and held back another sigh. "Not at all. I asked him to come aboard. To work with me. He wasn't interested. Jacob, on the other hand..."

"Jacob's the best rodeo man we have on the place. He could go all the way this year. I'm not pulling him off the circuit."

"Even if that's what he really wants?"

"Fool boy doesn't know what he wants."

There was no arguing with that tone, even though she was fairly sure Jacob knew exactly what he wanted. Lizzie knew the tone well and so she let the matter drop—for now. She would not pick a fight.

"Dad," she started again, "I can do this. I just need the go-ahead from you."

He rested his head back against the pillow. "I don't know, Lizzie. The rest of the board—they're old school. I'm not sure how they'll take to a woman sitting at the head of the table."

"I'm not just a woman. I'm a Baron. I have more at stake than any of them. The days of the old boys' club are over, Dad."

"Mark is the natural choice, as CFO," Brock continued, looking sideways at her.

"Are you trying to rile me up, Daddy? Because Mark Baker is a big old pain in my ass. He's the worst of the bunch."

"Why, because you asked him out and he refused?"

Her mouth opened and closed several times. "What?" she sputtered. "Who told you that?"

"Mark did, when he first came on at Baron. Thought it might be a problem. I didn't think it was, until now."

The rat bastard. Lizzie forgot about not rising to the bait and her temper heated. "That little weasel is a bald-faced liar. Truth is *he* asked *me* out when we were in college and *I* refused. He's so full of himself that he called me an icy bitch. You hired him the year before I finished school and he's been smug about it ever since I started in the HR department."

Brock smirked a little, somehow satisfied with her response. "I could use some of that water. The painkillers make my mouth dry."

She reached for the cup on the rolling table and handed it over. Brock adjusted the straw and took a long pull. "Ahhh," he said, handing the cup back. "So you gave him the brush-off. Interesting. Still, he's very good at his job."

"And so am I. And I'm family."

Brock pondered for a few moments. "It's a big responsibility, Liz," he finally said, serious once more. "And I'm not going to be out that long. Things will be fine."

"No, they won't," she argued. "Not to mention investor confidence. This needs to be decided and handled in the right way. Ask Julieta. She'll tell you the same thing—someone needs to be visible as leading the company. She can draft up a press release in no time."

"Then I can work from home."

Lizzie pressed her hands to her suddenly aching temples. "Dad, I know you'll have your laptop and video conferencing is a great thing, and we can definitely use those tools. But you won't be able to come to meetings for a while, and you're going to have physiotherapy appointments as well as tiring a little more easily. I'm asking you to trust me with this."

Brock looked away.

Lizzie's heart softened. "Look, I know you hate this. We all do. I also know you like to be in the thick of things. You're Brock Baron, right? Large and in charge. But you have to trust someone sometime." She pulled out the final weapon in her arsenal. "Can't you trust your own daughter?"

"I know you don't understand why I want Jet in the business," Brock said, his voice quieter now. "That has nothing to do with my confidence in you. You've never let me down, Lizzie. I know that."

Except she had. Because he was on the cusp of putting his faith in her and then she was going to have to tell him, one day soon, that she was accidentally pregnant and about to become a single mom. For Brock Baron, family was everything. He'd stepped in and raised them alone after Delia left. Then he'd adopted Peggy's boys and they were family even now that Peggy was gone. Same with Julieta and Alex. Brock was definitely all about the family unit and the two-parent home. Something that her baby wouldn't have.

She touched her lips, remembering Chris's kiss from this morning. If only things weren't quite so complicated where he was concerned.

"If I put you in the driver's seat, I don't want to be left in the dark or have any surprises. I want daily updates on what's happening and the status with projects."

What he wanted was his finger in every pie, but Lizzie hadn't really expected it to be any other way.

"Of course." Considering the loss of the recent contract, it wasn't an unreasonable request.

"And I'll be included in any board meetings and votes. If I can't make it to the office, I'll video from the ranch."

"That's fine, too."

He met her gaze. "Then consider yourself the interim president of Baron Energies."

The title and everything. Lizzie hadn't expected that. "Dad…"

"If the board's going to support you, they need to know I'm behind you 100 percent."

Oh, God. This was what she wanted, wasn't it? So why was she suddenly so terrified?

"I'll take care of it for you, I promise." She leaned forward and kissed his cheek.

"I'm not worried. I'm going to be with you every step of the way. And this isn't for very long. A few weeks, that's all."

That was the time frame Brock wanted, but Lizzie already knew the recovery could take longer than he expected. He thought he was invincible. That the rules didn't apply, but they did. Already their conversation had tired him. She could see it around his eyes and mouth, a look of strain and exhaustion.

"I'm going to go for now, but I'll check in tomorrow, okay?"

"Okay. Lizzie, first thing you should do is call a meeting for Monday morning and have Julieta draft a release…."

"I'll look after it. You just rest."

She kissed him again and left him in the hospital bed, looking vastly unhappy about the whole thing.

Lizzie wasn't so sure of herself either, but she'd fake it. She'd have to.

Chapter Five

By the time they reached San Antonio, Lizzie was exhausted. She'd done the driving this time, and during the extended moments of silence she'd begun planning a meeting agenda for Monday. When they'd stopped for gas, Chris had gotten out to pump and she'd sent two emails to Brock's executive assistant, Maria, copying in Julieta, who was head of the PR department, and Lizzie's own assistant, Emory, about the announcement and scheduling the meeting for Monday at 10:00 a.m.

With the hectic day before, and her restless sleep last night, knowing Chris was downstairs, the thought of another four hours of driving made her sigh. Perhaps she'd start back and get a hotel room for the night.

She parked at his condo, sliding into a visitor's spot. "I can't wait to have a shower and change my clothes," Chris commented, looking over at her. "Thanks for bringing me back."

"Thanks for going with me," she replied, smiling weakly. "This is going to sound weird, but it was good to have you there last night."

"You're not used to relying on other people," he guessed, one eyebrow raised.

She laughed a little. "Not really. I'm the oldest. I

think...well, everyone just expects me to handle things, and I do. But it can be a bit lonely."

What had prompted her to make such a confession? It must be the fatigue. Certainly not any growing intimacy between them.

"I think being the oldest must sometimes be like being an only child," he mused. "There's a lot of expectation involved. You don't want to let anyone down."

"Your parents are that way? Are they going to freak out about the baby, then? Be disappointed in you?"

He laughed, and once more she absorbed the pleasant sound. "Well, they'll wish I'd done it in the order you suggested earlier. But the thought of having a grandchild? They'll be over the moon."

She rested her hands on the steering wheel. "Can I ask you something?"

"Sure."

She swallowed, a little bit afraid if she were honest. "You were a little upset yesterday when I first told you, but you've done very little freaking out since. You're taking this remarkably in stride. Why don't you blame me more? Why aren't you angry? I've told you something that changes your life forever. Something you didn't choose."

He thought about his answer, a trait she admired. It was a good sign that he thought about his words instead of blurting things out without thinking. "It was an accident," he said quietly. "And it happened and it can't be changed, so being angry seems a bit counterproductive. As for why I'm not angry with you?" His gaze met hers. "I was the one who asked you back to my hotel room. I was the one who bought condoms from the vending machine in the bar bathroom—condoms which apparently failed at some point. And above all, what happened isn't this baby's fault either. Sometimes you have to play the cards you're dealt and it usually goes easier if you go with the current of the river instead of swimming against it."

"Easier said than done," she murmured.

"You're preaching to the choir," he answered, smiling ruefully. "Listen, it's midafternoon and you look whipped. You didn't stop for lunch. Why don't you come in and I'll order something to eat and you can refuel for the drive back."

"I shouldn't take up any more of your time," she answered. And yet the thought of putting the car in gear and driving for another four hours straight made her feel slightly limp. Then there was the fact that she had to pee. "Maybe I could come in and freshen up, get a drink," she suggested. "Just for a few minutes."

"Whatever."

The March sunshine was bright and soaked through her shirt, feeling good after the closed environment of her car. She shut her car door and gave a big stretch, then laughed. "I feel like a cat in the sun," she commented, stretching again. "Boy, that feels good."

Chris's dark gaze was burning into her again and she suddenly got self-conscious. "Lead on," she said, diverting her gaze and anchoring her purse strap on her shoulder.

There was no wait for the elevator and within seconds they were at Chris's door. He unlocked it and they stepped inside the quiet apartment. Lizzie noticed more today. Yesterday she'd been too nervous to register much of her surroundings. It wasn't a huge space, but it was clean and nicely decorated. The colors were warm, hues of browns and deep reds, and it felt homey even though it lacked a woman's touch in the little extras. Chris pointed her in the direction of the bathroom and she disappeared down the short hall.

When she came back, Chris was nowhere to be found. The door to the room at the end of the hall was closed—probably his bedroom, she realized, and the muffled sound of water running in the ensuite touched her ears. He'd said he was dying for a shower and clean clothes. She didn't want to leave without saying goodbye, so she went to the kitchen and got a drink of water and then sat down on the sofa to wait.

The cushions were very comfortable, and with the sound of the shower in the background, her eyelids grew heavy. *Just for a moment,* she thought, sliding down the cushions a bit more.

CHRIS HUNG UP his towel and turned off the light in the bathroom. The hot shower had felt good, and so did the clean jeans and T-shirt. He'd tried to be quick, knowing that Lizzie was still waiting, but he'd seen women "freshen up" before. He was probably done before she was.

Which made him quite surprised to find her sound asleep on his sofa, a soft curl of hair draped over her cheek and her lips slightly open.

God, she was beautiful. It was no wonder he'd temporarily lost his sanity that night.

He was glad he projected an image of calm about the situation. He'd gotten pretty good at that over the years, but on the inside he was still confused as hell. On one hand, he truly believed in having to play the hand he was dealt, just as he'd said. On the other, he was chafing at the bit. This year was his one chance to do something for himself. Now he was going to have to cut that short for yet another obligation.

And then of course he felt guilty for feeling resentful, like he was being completely selfish.

The truth was, he didn't really want to be an engineer any longer and it was time he faced it head-on. It wasn't that it was even a bad job. He had great coworkers, good benefits, steady employment and a really good paycheck. But it also didn't make him happy. His father had pushed for him to get an education, and he understood why. But to his mind, his father had had just about the best job ever in the world.

This year had been about more than goofing off, more than competing in rodeo. It had been a chance to see what life was like away from AB Windpower, to spend some time figuring out what he really wanted to do. Now, if he were to live up to his obligations, that chance was over. And yet not living up to his obligations was unthinkable.

While Lizzie slept, he grabbed the cordless phone, disappeared into the quiet kitchen and ordered pizza. Then he emailed AB's VP of Operations, Nicole Bennett, asking her to call him on Monday morning.

The buzzer at the lobby echoed through the quiet space and he jumped up, hurrying to answer it. He went down to pay for the food and when he came back up, Lizzie was stretching, her eyes still half closed from her nap.

The stretch had the same effect on him this time as it had before. Her shirt lifted, revealing a narrow band of skin and also accentuated the rounded curve of her breasts. Attraction? Hell yeah. That first night it had been purely physical, though they'd hit it off, too. Now there was more, and it didn't even have anything to do with the baby. He liked what he saw and who he saw. She was a good person. A bit driven, but smart and loyal and caring.

It only made her more attractive.

"I didn't mean to fall asleep." She bit down on her lip and it only served to draw his attention to her full, pink mouth.

He swallowed thickly. "You've had a crazy few days, not to mention the physical changes you must be experiencing. I ordered us in some pizza. I'm hungry." He smiled. "I wasn't sure what you liked, so I got one plain pepperoni and the other one loaded."

He put the boxes down on the dining table and she pushed herself up off the sofa, straightening her clothes. "Oh, my gosh, that smells good."

"You only had toast this morning and then a yogurt at the hospital. You must be starving."

"I could eat," she admitted, her cheeks pinking.

He got two plates while she opened the boxes. "There are black olives on this one. I think I love you."

He chuckled. "Loaded it is, then."

She slid the first piece onto her plate. "They're salty. For some reason they just taste so good right now."

"The spicy doesn't bother you?"

She shook her head. "Not so far. It's kind of weird what does and doesn't make me feel gross. Things I've always liked, I don't anymore. Other things I never ate are suddenly really appealing."

He put three large slices on his plate and sat down across from her. "Okay, so what sort of things do you like now that you didn't before?"

She ticked her fingers. "Hummus, asparagus, sweet potatoes."

"Hmm," he mused. "I like all of those. In fact I like pretty much everything. Of course, when I was growing up, I ate whatever was on the table. We couldn't afford for me to be picky."

"Black-eyed peas," Lizzie lamented, screwing up her

face. "Our housekeeper, Anna, made black-eyed peas and I hated them. And it didn't matter if we could afford it or not—we had to eat whatever was made for dinner." She smiled sadly. "It was like that when Mom was around, but she always found a way to make sure we had our favorites. After she left, things weren't so strict. Just having the family together for meals was enough, and Anna stepped in and looked after us. And then when Dad married Peggy, it was really good again."

"Your mother left you?"

"Yeah, when Jet was little."

Chris tried to imagine that. How could a mother just walk away from her four kids?

Lizzie finished the first piece of pizza and reached for another. "This is so good. I didn't realize how hungry I was."

"You need to make sure you eat. That taking care of yourself thing." She wasn't going to do anyone any good if she was tired and weak.

"Yes, Mom," she joked. He noticed the color was back in her cheeks and her hair looked soft and slightly mussed from the nap. He liked it.

When his first two slices of pizza were gone, he wiped his fingers on a paper napkin and sat back. "Lizzie, I want to be involved. I know it'll be hard from here, but you've got enough on your plate that I don't want you to feel like you're all alone."

She looked startled at his words and put down her pizza. "Oh. Well, I won't be alone. I'll have Savannah and Carly and Julieta, won't I?"

"Except they don't know about the baby."

"Right."

"And you're going to be busy running Baron, too."

"What are you suggesting, Chris?"

He didn't blame her for looking wary. "I'm not sure, and I'm going to need a few days to think, but will you at least call me and let me know how you're doing? I'd like to come to a doctor's appointment, too, if I can. Is there anything you need?"

She shook her head. "The only thing I need right now is to eat well, get lots of sleep, take my vitamins."

He got up and grabbed a notepad and pen from the kitchen. "Here are my numbers." He jotted them down. "This is my phone here at the condo, and this is my cell which is probably more reliable. And this is my email address. You can text or email or phone anytime, day or night, okay?"

He tore the sheet off the tablet and held it out.

"Thanks." She took it and then wiggled her fingers for the paper. "I should do the same for you. My cell and my office. The two best places to reach me."

He found it odd she didn't include her home number, but whatever.

She pushed her plate away. "This was great, but I should be going. Thanks for the rest stop. I needed the nap and the food, I guess."

"Anytime," he answered, but it made things awkward as they both knew it wasn't possible to pop in at random since they lived so far apart.

She got up from the table and picked up her purse from the end of the sofa. "I guess I'll drop in and see Dad before visitors' hours are over tonight, and tomorrow I'll work out the board meeting I've arranged for Monday. Wish me luck."

She smiled at him then, and he saw something new in her. Vulnerability. For all her confidence, she wasn't as sure of herself as she led people to believe.

He went forward and, against his better judgment,

folded her into his arms. "You'll do great," he murmured against her hair.

She was stiff for a few seconds and then she relaxed, her hands resting on Chris's shoulders as she softened into his embrace. "I hope so."

Having her close, pressed up against him was igniting the attraction again. It would be so easy to slide his mouth over hers, to press her body more firmly into his, maybe even carry her into his bedroom and make love to her again. There was no denying the chemistry that still sizzled between them.

But he did the right thing and put his hands on her arms, pushing her away a little and pasting on what he hoped looked like a platonic smile. "You've got a bit of a drive. Text me when you get there, okay?"

"You're not going to get all overprotective, are you?" Her dark, mysterious eyes gazed up into his and he felt himself slipping.

"I just want to know when you're there safe and sound, that's all."

"I'll text you."

"You want some pizza for the road?"

Their bodies still hovered close together. "Honestly," she murmured, "you don't have to look after me. I'm a big girl."

He leaned forward and kissed her forehead—the safest area of her face. Then he opened the front door, let her out, and closed it again behind her.

He pressed his forehead to the door and exhaled heavily. She was right. He didn't have to look after her. And damn it all anyway, because even though he didn't have to, he wanted to.

And that probably wasn't good at all.

Chapter Six

Lizzie rested her elbows on her desk and her forehead against her fingers. Thank God *that* was over. She'd just managed to chair her first board meeting without messing things up too badly. She'd been right. Mark Baker wasn't thrilled with her sitting in the big chair, but support had come from a few unexpected sources, giving her a boost.

Emory, her assistant, knocked discreetly on the door. "Hey, Lizzie? You want some lunch?"

Her stomach rumbled. Maria, Brock's executive assistant, had thought to have a selection of muffins on hand along with coffee for the meeting. Lizzie had stuck with water, but the blueberry wheat muffin had kept her full enough to ward off any lingering nausea.

"I'd love a turkey sandwich, Em."

"I'll be back soon."

Emory shut the door quietly behind her. Rather than move into Brock's larger office, Lizzie had decided to stay in her own space. Maria was only down the hall if she needed anything anyway.

She was skimming a resume for a new engineer—someone named Jasmine Carter—when her phone buzzed. She looked down to see an incoming text message. One click told her it was from Chris.

How did the meeting go?

She held the phone in both hands and typed with her thumbs.

Meh. As good as could be expected. The predicted resistance though some support too. There were muffins.

Do you ever think of anything other than food?

Yes. Sleep.

She imagined him smiling on the other end.

LOL

She shouldn't be enjoying the simple messages so much, but they were a bright spot in her day. She had two more meetings this afternoon and tonight she would be back at the hospital to give Brock an update. But this break helped her wind down a little bit.

I got the date for my next checkup. It's two weeks from tomorrow at four o'clock.

Will you hear the heartbeat or anything?

Maybe. I'll be over ten weeks by then.

Over ten weeks. Soon after that, she'd have to finally tell her family. Her clothes wouldn't fit forever, and with her usual power suits and fitted outfits, a change in wardrobe would be noticeable. Besides, then she'd be past the first trimester.

I could come with you—if you want.

Oh my. She imagined being examined with Chris in the room and was sure she'd be embarrassed. But then she imagined hearing her baby's heartbeat all alone and it didn't feel right. It seemed right to share it with someone, and who else but the baby's father?

You sure you want to make the drive?

There was a bit of a pause between messages, but finally a reply came.

No biggie. I'll be there. Just text me the address.

Emory knocked and came in bearing Lizzie's sandwich and a bottle of water. "Thanks, Em," she said, smiling, and checked her watch. Just enough time to eat and get ready for her next meeting.

Lunch is here. GTG. TTYL.

C U soon, he replied.

She tucked the phone away and unwrapped her sandwich. She was looking forward to seeing him—perhaps too much.

CHRIS STEPPED INTO the coffee shop and scanned the customers. There she was, her dark brown hair tucked up in a no-nonsense bun, clicking away on her smartphone. One thing he could say about Nicole Bennett—she was one hell of a hard worker. She was a one-woman dynamo, always at the forefront of anything happening with the company. Everyone knew she was Adele Black's right hand at AB Windpower.

He grabbed a plain black coffee from the barista and made his way over to her table. "Hey, thanks for meeting me," he said, pulling out a chair. "I could have come into the office."

Nicole looked up and smiled, putting down her phone. "That's okay. I like to get out of the office now and again. And it gives me an excuse to grab a chocolate pecan bar."

The empty paper wrapper sat under her coffee cup.

"So," she said, picking up her beverage, "you're looking to come back to work already. Rodeo not all you expected?" She took a sip, a curious expression on her face as she asked him the question.

"Actually, the rodeo's been great." Too great. The more he thought about it the more he knew this was the right thing but he was choked that he was going to miss the rest of the season. "Something's come up, is all."

"Yeah, earning a living wage is kind of important, huh." She grinned again. "And you won't hear complaints from us anyway. I know Adele gave you the leave because she wanted to keep you happy and make sure you came back. She was thrilled when I told her you'd called."

Which should have made him happy. Instead all he felt was locked in, inside a career he didn't truly want.

"Nothing's written in stone yet, Nicole." He blew on his coffee before taking a hot sip. "I was wondering if there's any chance to work somewhere other than San Antonio. If there's anything closer to the Dallas–Fort Worth area." He'd thought about it all day yesterday and figured at least that way he'd be a bit closer to his kid. He was pretty sure Lizzie had no plans to leave Baron and her family and move this way, and really, why would she?

Nicole met his gaze evenly. "You turned down the management offer before."

Management. Talk about being locked in even more. At least in his position here, he'd been out in the field some of the time. It wasn't the same thing day in and day out. If he moved into something supervisory, those opportunities would be gone.

Then again, he'd be in a more secure position to be a dad. He kept thinking what his own father would say. And it would center around providing the best life possible for his kid. That's what his dad had done for him, and without the benefit of the education Chris had. Didn't his kid deserve the same?

"It would depend on the position," he responded cautiously.

"We're still looking for someone to manage a satellite office in Dallas. I know you didn't want to be that far from your family before, so what's changed?"

They hadn't told anyone about the baby yet and he wasn't about to tell Nicole before they'd even announced it to family. "Some personal circumstances," he answered cryptically.

"Well, it'd be a bump in salary for you. You'd head up the office there, manage the engineers and technicians for our local interests. Right now we have an admin assistant there who is reporting to head office, but it's not the most efficient way to run it. It needs someone on site. Anything to do with head office can be done over the phone. And you'd have to travel here a little, for meetings, but that would be minimal. You'd be our front person in that part of the state."

She took a napkin and wrote a number down on it.

"This is the salary offer. The benefits package is a little nicer, as well. I can email you those details."

His eyes nearly bugged out of his head. When they'd first approached him about the job, he hadn't even considered it. He wanted the year off and he wanted to be close to his parents, not have to move. This was a good offer. A damned good offer. And he could drive to see his mom and dad now and again, especially if he had a son or daughter to take with him.

A son or daughter. Sometimes thinking about that still freaked him out, made his chest tighten and his heart race. He was so not ready for fatherhood!

"Can I have a few days to think about it?"

She smiled. "Of course you can."

Her coffee was gone and she reached down for her bag. "I've got to get back to the office for a meeting. It's kind of an exciting time to be in energy. And hey, when you're in Dallas you'll be in the heart of it. What do you hear about Baron Energies these days?"

It was too casual a question for it to not be intentional. His eyes narrowed. "Why? I've met the brothers before. They're a big rodeo family, as well as being in the oil business."

"Just curious. There was a press release this morning about Brock Baron being injured late last week and being out of commission for a while. His daughter, Elizabeth, is taking over. Do you know her?"

His throat felt tight. "A little."

"It'll be interesting to see how she handles being at the helm—if she's a Daddy's girl with a token position or if she can really stand the heat. They lost a big contract not long ago."

The words to defend Lizzie rose to his tongue but he wisely refrained. "Knowing that family, you'd be smart not to underestimate them," he advised. "What's the big interest all of a sudden? They're oil. We're alternative energy."

Nicole shrugged. "It's interesting, that's all. Besides, Elizabeth has publicly said that she's interested in other energy alternatives."

It still felt a little off, but Nicole got up and patted his shoulder. "Give me a call later this week and let me know what you've decided. The space is there, we'd just need to order furniture for your office, that sort of thing."

"Thanks. I'll call you soon."

She shouldered her bag and maneuvered around the tables in the café on her way out while Chris sat and pondered the offer. Under the circumstances it was the perfect solution. And really, what had he expected? This year was supposed to be a onetime leave. It wasn't a life plan, so why was he letting it bum him out so much?

He'd do some thinking, make a few arrangements and talk to Lizzie when he went to Dallas for her doctor's appointment.

DOCTOR MENDEZ'S OFFICE was like any other medical office in America: pastel walls covered in prints, coffee tables with magazines, pamphlets in a display and several patients waiting on vinyl chairs while the phone rang incessantly.

Lizzie shifted in her chair. At ten weeks she wasn't discernibly pregnant, though quite often lately she'd found herself undoing her trousers or skirt button. The morning sickness hadn't abated either, and she was getting rather tired of the morning routine of throwing up before she even made it to the shower.

She checked her watch again—it was three-twenty-seven and her appointment was for three-thirty and no sign of Chris. He'd said he was coming in his text yesterday, but as each minute ticked by she wasn't so sure of him.

Their first...well, second, really...weekend together had gone far better than she'd imagined, but that had been two weeks ago. Maybe he'd changed his mind. Maybe it would be easier for everyone if he did.

The door opened and he stepped through, all windswept hair and plaid shirt and jeans paired with scuffed but clean boots.

Easier, maybe. But she couldn't deny that she was glad to see him just the same.

"Sorry I'm late," he said, sitting down beside her. "I took a wrong turn, and then I had a hard time finding parking. I'm not as familiar with Dallas as I should be."

"It's okay. I haven't been called in yet, and I think she's running a little late anyway."

He let out a breath and leaned back in his chair. "So... how're you feeling?"

"Fat," she answered, sounding distinctly grumpy.

He laughed. "You're not even showing yet, and you feel fat?"

"Maybe I'm not showing, but I'm outgrowing my clothes. My waistbands, at least. Which makes me *feel* fat."

He didn't say anything, so she looked over at him and caught him smiling at her, his arms folded across his chest. "What?" she asked.

"You look great," he said. "So don't worry about it."

"Charmer," she muttered under her breath, and he surprised her again by chuckling.

"Hey, if we're in this together, it's probably easier if we get along. Right?"

"Yes, but do you have to be so nice about it?"

Again he laughed. "Relax, Lizzie."

"Elizabeth Baron?"

They looked up in unison at the nurse standing by the desk. "That's me," she whispered, picking up her purse.

"Do you want me to… That is…"

"I'll get her to bring you in at the end, okay?"

He looked relieved. "Okay."

She followed the nurse to the exam room and was surprised that she didn't have to put on a gown. "Just remove your pants," the nurse suggested. "We'll try to hear a fetal heartbeat today, but there are no guarantees. Sometimes we can't hear it for another few weeks."

After the nurse went out, Lizzie removed her trousers and draped them over a chair, and then lay down on the exam table and pulled up the light cotton sheet. Moments later Dr. Mendez came in carrying Lizzie's chart and offering a friendly smile.

"How're you feeling?" she asked warmly. "Still morning sick?"

"Unfortunately."

"All day long or just in the mornings?"

"Just in the mornings, thank goodness."

Dr. Mendez looked over her glasses at Lizzie. "I can give you an anti-nauseant, which will help, or we can just let it run its course. As long as you're getting enough nutrition."

"I eat like a horse after ten o'clock," she admitted. "And I'm craving fruit and cucumbers."

"Not bad things to crave at all," the doctor agreed. "Let's let it go for now then, if you can handle it, and if you're still sick at your next appointment, revisit it."

"Sounds good to me."

"Right—let's take your blood pressure."

They went through the rest of the appointment, talking about symptoms and fetal development and what Lizzie could expect over the next few weeks. "Now we can check for the heartbeat. No promises, but I usually find my patients find things very real once they hear it. It's a special kind of moment."

Lizzie's heart quickened just thinking about it. "The baby's father is in the waiting room. I think he'd like to be here for this."

"Let's bring him in then, by all means."

"His name is Chris. Chris Miller."

Moments later Chris was ushered into the room, looking way more out of place than he had before. She smiled tentatively at him, suddenly feeling very exposed even though the sheet covered her to the waist. It seemed stupid considering he'd seen her naked before, seeing they'd made this baby together. But this was a whole other situation. That night had been fantasy. This was reality, and a rather big dose of it all at once.

"Mr. Miller, you can stand right here." Dr. Mendez made room by Lizzie's shoulder while the nurse arranged everything. Before Lizzie had time to think, the sheet was tucked down and the waistband of her panties was pulled down, as well. There was no time for modesty; before she could register any embarrassment the instrument touched her skin.

She flinched, unprepared for the cold gel on the Doppler as the doctor moved it around her pelvis, searching for a heartbeat. Chris's hand cupped her shoulder, his fingers digging in slightly and she realized she was holding her breath, waiting. The doctor's forehead puckered as she frowned. "I'm not sure we're going to get this today. It is a little early. Let's give it one more try."

She shifted it twice more and then suddenly there it was, the bum-bump sound of it filling the room and Lizzie's ears. Dr. Mendez smiled and Lizzie felt tears form in her eyes. "Oh, my gosh," she whispered, her smile so wide she wondered if her face might split. "Oh, my gosh."

Chris's hand was tight on her shoulder now. "Listen to that," he said, his voice full of awe. "It sounds like hoofbeats."

"Oh, you and your horses," she teased him. She listened a little more, loving the sound. Chris leaned over, just a little, and pressed a warm kiss on her forehead.

"One-forty, right in there," Dr. Mendez said, removing the Doppler and saving Lizzie from further emotional upheaval as Chris stepped back. The sound was gone and the nurse gave Lizzie a tissue to wipe the gel off her belly. "It looks like everything is going right on schedule. Congratulations."

"Thanks," Lizzie said, still awestruck.

"You're free to go now. I want to see you in another four weeks, unless you need to reach me sooner. And Lizzie, I know you're working very hard these days. Take time to put your feet up, and make sure you eat properly. You have to take care of yourself first and foremost."

"I'll make sure she does," Chris promised.

When they were alone, Lizzie balled up the tissue, pulled up her panties and sat up. "You'll make sure? And how do you propose to do that?" As if she needed help. As if she'd take orders.

"I wanted to talk to you about that. How about you let me buy you both dinner tonight to celebrate?"

At least he didn't suggest going to her apartment. "Just dinner? And what are we celebrating?"

"Just dinner," he promised, crossing his heart. The action made him look like an adorable schoolboy. "To celebrate a healthy baby, of course. Wherever you want to go."

"Marinelli's." She stated her favorite Italian restaurant that was also on the pricey side. "I've got a craving for veal parmesan and tiramisu."

And she wondered why her waistbands weren't fitting properly anymore....

She'd also taken perverse pleasure in naming somewhere that his jeans and plaid cotton would be entirely inappropriate. Why had she done that? Did she really need to be in control so much?

She didn't like the answer that came a little too quickly to her mind.

"That sounds great. I'll call and make a reservation and then text with a time I'll pick you up, how does that sound?"

He was being too agreeable. "Don't worry about it. It's a bit on the fancy side. We can do something a little more casual. Could you hand me my pants, please?"

She held out her hand and waggled her fingers.

He picked up her pants and handed them over. She swung her legs over the side of the bed and pulled them on, hopping down and sucking in as best she could so he wouldn't see her fighting with the button.

"Fancy's fine. I haven't had Italian in a while. It sounds good."

He went to the door and held it open for her. She swept through, stopping at the desk to make her next appointment. To her surprise, Chris asked the receptionist to give him an appointment card as well, and he tucked it into his wallet.

Once outside the office, Lizzie kept her voice low. "You don't have to come every time, you know."

"I know that. But I'd like to know when they are, just the same. Elevator or stairs?"

"Stairs. I plan on eating well tonight."

"You are eating for two after all."

She rolled her eyes.

They didn't talk as they went down the stairs, and once outside she realized they were parked in different rows.

"Marinelli's, right? That's what you said?"

"Yes."

"And give me your address again. In case I get lost. I'll put it in my GPS."

She gave him the street address and he nodded. "Right. See you tonight then. I'll text the time."

"Chris?" He'd started to walk away and she found herself missing his company already. That was foolish. Having him around was the exception, not the rule. And yet she found that most days she felt very strange and isolated, going through the pregnancy alone. "Thanks for coming today. I'm glad you were there."

His eyes warmed. "I'm glad I was, too. See you soon, Liz."

He'd called her Liz, not Lizzie, she realized, and coming from Chris it sounded nearly like an endearment. She'd always been Lizzie and it was fine, but sometimes she longed for something a bit more grown up. That was why she'd told him her name was Elizabeth the first night, using the long version. She liked his shortened version just as well, she found.

He walked away and she took in the view of faded back pockets and broad shoulders.

Hooo boy, she sure was in trouble. Because things between them were far from over. And tap-dancing around this was like running through a pasture full of cow patties. She was pretty sure that sooner or later, she was going to step in it.

Chapter Seven

The text message said that he'd pick her up at six-thirty, and at six o'clock she was still deliberating on what to wear. In a very strange way this felt like a first date—she and Chris seemed determined to do everything backwards. Currently four dresses were draped over her bedspread and she was staring critically in the mirror at the small pouch that had formed just below her waistline. She put her hands on it, dressed in only her underwear, and marveled again that a life thrived beneath her fingers. A life with a beating heart that had been loud and clear just this afternoon.

It had been amazing and it had been terrifying. With each passing day she was getting more used to the idea of being a mom. More…excited. Not only was it a new and unexpected feeling, she'd been thinking about her own mother more often. She imagined that the emotions she was feeling now—a special kind of love—would only increase when the baby was born.

How could a mother just walk away from that? How could she not come back, as if her kids didn't matter?

Lizzie couldn't imagine doing such a thing. And yet deep down she knew it happened because she'd seen it. She'd lived it. She wondered what had changed in her mom to make her want to leave her family behind. The only thing she could come up with was postpartum depression, though she'd never breathed a word of her suspicion to her siblings. It seemed the topic of Delia Baron was a no-go zone. Now that Lizzie was expecting her own baby, she was starting to be afraid that maybe it would happen to her, too—and she had no one to talk to about it.

She checked her watch and saw that it was nearly six-fifteen. She had to choose a dress and get it over with. In the end she went with a black jersey wrap style, the stretch of the fabric comfortable, the black slimming and the folds of the skirt a good camouflage for the pod at her middle. The deep V of the neckline looked better than usual, thanks to another pregnancy symptom that had resulted in better cleavage. She paired the dress with a smart pair of black heels and fastened a string of pearls around her neck. There. A little bit sexy, a little bit classy. Entirely appropriate for dinner.

Her bell rang at six twenty-nine—goodness, Chris had a habit of being punctual—and she opened the door to find him in a suit and tie. Her lips dropped open at the sight of him, looking so different out of his jeans and T-shirts and boots. The suit was a good one, dark gray and well-fitting through his shoulders and hips, and his tie was red, with geometric squares in a simple pattern. He was perfect right down to the tips of his dust-free shoes.

"At a loss for words?" he asked with a smile.

"You look… That's a nice suit." She stumbled over the compliment.

"Thanks. You didn't think I had one, did you?"

Her cheeks heated. "You don't seem the type."

"A man should always have a good suit."

"For weddings and funerals?"

He smiled again. "And dates with beautiful women."

Lizzie tried to remain immune to the compliment. She leaned forward and whispered, "Hey, you don't have to do that sort of thing with me. Clearly your charm already worked."

"It's the truth. Now, are you ready to go?"

"Just let me grab my purse." She took a beaded clutch from the counter and grabbed her keys. In the parking lot he opened the door of his truck for her and she climbed in, not really minding taking it instead of her car. It was a relatively new half-ton with power everything and comfortable seats. He reset the address for the restaurant in the GPS and they were on their way.

"You look nice tonight," he offered, stopping at a traffic light. "I like your hair that way."

She'd left it down, pulling a few strands back from the sides and anchoring them with bobby pins while the rest of her hair fell in slight waves over her shoulders. She rarely wore it like this; at work she went for something more no-nonsense and out at the ranch it was usually in a practical long ponytail.

The evening was starting to feel very special indeed.

At the restaurant she was delighted to discover that their table was in a back corner, quiet and cozy with candlelight and soft music. They were given menus and before they even had them opened, waitstaff arrived with a basket of warm, fragrant bread and a chilled bottle of cider.

Despite her best intentions, she had to admit she was being romanced, and she liked it. When was the last time she'd been treated this special? She couldn't quite remember.

Chris held up his glass. "We got off to a very unusual start," he admitted. "But you were right. We should begin as we mean to go on. To a healthy baby boy or girl and his or her bright future."

Her vision blurred and she blinked. How lovely and generous of him. Tonight was a far cry from tequila shots at a honky-tonk and a discount motel room.

She raised her glass. "Thank you, Christopher," she said softly, touching the rim to his in a faint tinkle.

The cider was tart and refreshing and Lizzie helped herself to a piece of bread, dipping it in fragrant olive oil and balsamic vinegar. A waiter came and took their order and disappeared again, and Lizzie began to enjoy herself. It was a good date. Even if it wasn't supposed to be romantic, it was still relaxing and special and a complete treat. Way better than takeout on the way home from the office or a warmed-up frozen dinner at the end of a long day.

"Lizzie, I wanted to talk to you about something," Chris began, putting down his glass. "I told you I wanted some time to think about things and how involved I wanted to be, and I've done that."

The relaxed feeling went away and Lizzie's body tensed. Was he going to start making demands now? She knew what she was going to do. She was going to have this baby and be a mom. She'd stay on at Baron and hire a nanny, and she'd spend as much time as possible with her son or daughter.

"You know I don't care about child support," she reminded him. The less she demanded of him, the less he could demand of her, right?

"I appreciate that, but I intend to support my kid, financially and otherwise," he stated calmly.

"Otherwise?"

"Lizzie, I intend to be a father to my child. I can't go on with my life, pretending that he or she doesn't exist."

Her lips twisted…the last thing she wanted for her baby was to be carted back and forth between houses and all the confusion and insecurity that could come from that sort of relationship.

"I just want my baby to have stability and consistency, and I'm worried that won't happen if we bounce her back and forth, you know?" She fiddled with her napkin.

"You mean you're worried you won't have parental control twenty-four seven?"

Was that it? Was it really a control issue? She pursed her lips, unsure of how to answer.

He sighed. "If you were in my position, could you simply pretend that your child didn't exist? It's not all about obligation. It's about…" He broke off, clearly having as much trouble coming up with the right words as she was.

"It's about what?" she asked quietly.

It took him a while to form his answer. "However this baby was conceived doesn't matter. That's about us, not him or her. I don't want my child wondering why his father doesn't care enough to be a part of his life. I do care. I care already. You want stability and security? I want that, too, and it has little to do with splitting time between two houses. It has to do with caring and attention. Your mother walked out on you, and you know how much that hurt. Can you honestly say it would be better for our baby if I walked away?"

He'd used her mother against her, and it hurt. It also stung that he was so right.

"I'm scared," she admitted.

"So am I," he answered, but she shook her head.

"No, you don't understand." She took a hasty sip of cider; her throat felt suddenly dry. "I'm afraid I won't be a good parent. That you'll be better than me. That maybe he or she will…" She swallowed against a lump in her throat. "Will love you more than me." Oh, how horrible that sounded! She wasn't generally so insecure. And yes, she was competitive, but not for affection. What on earth was wrong with her?

"Lizzie." He reached out for her hand. "No one is born knowing how to be a parent. I'm pretty sure about that. You're a strong, independent woman. You're smart and when you relax a little you can even be funny." He squeezed her fingers. "You're going to be a fine mom, because you want to be. You're already trying so hard. How can you possibly fail?"

He looked into her eyes. "And I'll be there to help."

It was so dangerous when he looked at her that way, all serious and honest, and it made her go all melty, which wouldn't help the situation at all. She wanted to believe him so badly, have the same faith in herself as he did. "How can you say that? You live in another city."

He sat back, sliding his hand away from hers. "That's what I wanted to talk to you about. I spoke to my bosses about going back to work."

"And cut short your leave of absence?" She was feeling worse and worse now. From what he'd told her, he'd really looked forward to this year and doing what he wanted. "You don't need to do that."

"I think I do. Anyway, they need someone to head up the local office. It's a promotion for me and it would mean I'd be in the Dallas area. Closer to you and the baby."

Her mouth dropped open. "You'd move here?"

He nodded. "To be honest, they approached me with the job last year and I turned it down, because I was already planning my leave."

"But you were really enjoying it. And doing better, from looking at the standings." She'd checked. His last few outings he'd been pretty competitive. After so long away, she wondered how good he'd be if he dedicated more time to it, like Jacob and Jet. He could be a real contender.

He shrugged, but for once he didn't meet her eyes. "It was just me being a little self-indulgent anyway," he answered.

She was going to press him about that but the waiter arrived with their food and spent several moments offering fresh pepper and parmesan and ensuring everything was just right.

When they were finally alone again, Lizzie picked up her fork. "I don't want you to feel like you have to turn your life upside down for this."

"I'm not," he assured her. "Like I said, it was a year of goofing off. It's not a big deal."

But she could tell by the way he wouldn't meet her eyes that it was. She picked up her knife and it slid through her tender veal like it was butter. She tried to eat normally, savoring the meat, pasta and marinara but it was awkward. He *was* turning his whole life upside down for this. And he was doing it because he was putting their child first—a child that wasn't even born yet.

She remembered the look of wonder in his eyes when they'd heard the heartbeat today and the tender way he'd kissed her forehead.

Oh dear. She was in so much trouble here and it wasn't all to do with being pregnant.

"I think you're going to be a very good father," she said quietly, putting down her fork.

He met her gaze over the flickering candles. "If I am, it's because I had a good example at home. I know that my dad sacrificed for me and always wanted the best for me, and that's what I want for my children, too."

Children. She dropped her gaze to her food and picked up her fork again, surprised by her sudden reaction to that word. It really hit home then that they'd be coparenting but still having separate lives. He'd likely meet someone and marry her and have another family, and that woman would be her baby's stepmother. And maybe she'd marry and have more babies, too...though for some reason, while she could see Chris surrounded by kids and a beautiful wife and the perfect life, she couldn't quite envision that for herself.

This was always going to be complicated, wasn't it?

"Liz? Is your food okay?"

"It's delicious." She smiled and made a show of taking another bite of veal parmesan.

"Hey." She looked up to find him watching her, his fork paused midair holding a square of ravioli. "Remember what we said from the beginning. One day at a time and we'll figure all this out. It's going to be fine."

She wished she had his confidence, but his easy manner and earnest eyes had her nearly believing him.

"Now, come on," he urged. "Relax and eat your dinner. Because there's tiramisu still to come." He popped the ravioli into his mouth.

By the end of the meal there was still pasta left on Lizzie's plate and she sat back, completely full. "I adore tiramisu, but I don't think I can eat another bite."

When the waiter came to remove their plates, Chris smiled up at him. "Could we have two orders of tiramisu to go, please?"

"Certainly, sir," he answered, disappearing once more.

"You didn't have to do that," she said, toying with her napkin.

"It's my favorite," Chris shrugged. "And I know you

like it, too. Just put it in your fridge. Or, if I know you, you'll have room once you get home."

"I doubt it," she answered, patting her tummy.

"Wanna bet?" He grinned at her. "I noticed that you eat often, but you don't eat a lot at a time. I did some reading and it said that sometimes eating smaller meals more frequently helps with the nausea."

She wasn't sure what was more shocking—the fact that he'd read up on pregnancy or that he'd noticed her eating habits. "The doctor said that should go away in a few more weeks. I have my fingers crossed."

"I'm sure."

The waiter came back with their desserts and the bill. Chris tucked a credit card in the leather folder and handed it back. When it had run through, he signed his copy and nodded at Lizzie. "Are you ready?"

"Yes."

He carried the box of dessert and as they went through the door to the restaurant, his hand rested on the curve of her spine just for a moment until they were outside. The evening had cooled and Lizzie found herself wishing she'd worn a wrap with the dress, but seeing Chris in his suit and tie had fried her brain and she'd forgotten.

"It's a bit chilly," he observed. "Are you cold?"

"I'm fine." They were nearly to the truck but he stopped, handed her the box, and took off his suit coat.

"Here, this should help." He draped it over her shoulders and took the box back before starting across the last row of the parking lot.

The jacket was still warm from his body as it clung to her shoulders, and the scent of his aftershave surrounded her. Good heavens, he smelled good. Not only that, but without the jacket on she could see how his shoulders were broad in the crisp white shirt and tapered to his narrow waist and hips, tucked into his trousers.

Cowboy Chris was incredibly sexy. She'd found him so that first night, and since then, too, in his plaid shirts and jeans. But he could equally pull off the professional look and she was afraid the attraction she felt for him was in no danger of dying off. Thank goodness he hadn't clued in to how strongly she reacted to him, or pressed the issue. He hadn't, not since the kiss that first weekend in her condo.

He opened her door and she hopped in, and when he got in he put the cake on the seat between them.

"So when do you start your new job?" Lizzie curled deeper into the comfort of his jacket. The near-darkness outside along with the softly playing radio made it rather cozy in the cab of the truck.

"Monday. I've spent this week getting things in order in San Antonio, and went out to my mom and dad's for a few days."

She looked over at him. "Did you tell them?"

He took his eyes off the road for a moment. "No." He looked straight ahead again, but kept talking. "I wanted to. Nearly did, but you and I hadn't talked about saying anything to anyone and I didn't think I should without discussing it with you first. So I just told them I'd been offered this job. They were disappointed at me being farther away, but happy for me."

They were going to have to say something soon and she knew it. There was only so long she could manage to avoid the topic before people started asking questions. Her declining a drink at a social event, leaving the office for doctor appointments, the few times she'd stood up and been light-headed and had to pause to regain her equilibrium. Carly had stopped by the office once on her way back to Houston and brought coffee. Rather than explain, Lizzie had taken a few stomach-turning sips and then faked her way through the visit.

She just couldn't imagine what the right time would be. Brock was home and grouchy because he was virtually immobile, and he picked apart her daily reports and added so much input that she knew he didn't trust her in the job yet.

She sighed—loudly.

"Tired?"

She smiled halfheartedly and laughed a little. "Always."

When they got back to her complex, he left the truck running but got out to open her door. She slid out but came a little too fast, rolling one of her heels, and his arms reached out to steady her.

The touch burned through his jacket sleeve straight to her skin. "Thanks," she breathed.

He reached inside and handed her the pastry box. "Here you go."

She looked up at him. "But your piece is in here, too."

"That's okay. You can have one now and save the other for later."

Trouble was, she didn't want the evening to end just yet. She shrugged off his suit coat and handed it back to him. "Thanks for the jacket."

"You're welcome."

The evening air bit at her shoulders again and she knew she should get inside, but still she hesitated. "Where are you staying, Chris?"

His gaze burned into hers as he answered. "At a motel not too far from the office. I have a kitchenette and everything. I'm renting it by the week until I find something more permanent."

That didn't sound too exciting to her. She took a breath and said what she really wanted to and the hell with it. "Do you want to come up and have your dessert? It's not fair for me to take both pieces."

"You're sure?"

"Why not?"

After she said it she knew there were tons of reasons why he shouldn't. They were supposed to keep this businesslike. This would blur the lines. She still had these nagging feelings for him. It was late. He smelled good. And so on…

"I'd like that," he answered, and he jumped into the truck and shut off the ignition, pocketing the keys.

The door slammed behind her as she led the way to the front doors, his footsteps sounding behind her.

Chapter Eight

Chris's stomach was a bundle of nerves as he waited for Lizzie to open her door. Tonight had been good. Too good at times. There'd been moments of tension but other moments where their eyes had met and he'd known. Spending the night with her hadn't been an accident. It felt an awful lot like fate. Something he'd never truly believed in before, but the more time they spent together the more it felt like something beyond his control was engineering his life.

He was bothered especially by the fact that he should be more upset about it than he was. And yet he wasn't. Somehow being here tonight, with a pastry box of tiramisu, felt strangely inevitable.

The door swung open and they stepped inside. Lizzie hit a switch and the living room was bathed in warm light from the ornate wall sconces. There was the sofa where he'd slept the last time he'd been in town. The efficient kitchen where they'd shared toast and one not-quite-satisfactory kiss.

"Come on in," she said, and to his surprise she kicked off her heels and left them by the door. She took her box of dessert to the kitchen. "You were right. I have room now." She smiled up at him wickedly as she put the box on the breakfast counter and opened a cupboard door for plates.

He draped his jacket over an armchair and took a steadying breath. It was just dessert. Except right now she looked impossibly young and innocent with her hair down and the anticipation of the creamy confection written all over her face. How could a man expect to remain immune to that? Added into it that she was carrying his child and he wasn't sure what he was supposed to do.

"I don't have coffee, sorry. This should probably be eaten with a good cup of espresso."

"And then I'd lay awake half the night," he replied, stepping forward and accepting the plate she offered. "Know what would really taste good with it?"

She looked up and he was hit with it again. That sense of rightness that scared the living hell out of him.

"What?"

"Milk. You got any of that in the fridge? Good, cold milk."

She laughed. "That I've got. Boy, we're really exciting, aren't we? Sparkling cider and milk on our big date."

The milk jug was in her hand, halfway to the countertop when she realized what she'd said and started to blush. "I didn't mean it as a date date," she stammered.

"Would it be so bad? Being on a date with me?"

The blush deepened. "Um...of course not. It's just that it would complicate things. Haven't we had this conversation already?"

She regained her composure and got out two glasses, but he noticed her hand shook slightly as she was pouring the milk.

So what the hell did he want from her? It was as though she had two faces. The first face was that of the mother of his kid. He saw that woman and knew that they both had to step up and act like responsible expecting parents. And then there was the other face, which was that of a beautiful, smart woman. A woman he was still attracted to. A woman he couldn't get out of his mind. Putting the two together made an ungodly mess he couldn't begin to sort out. If he pursued anything it would only mess up the parenting side of things.

But ignoring the way they looked at each other, the way his pulse seemed to quicken the moment he saw her, the way it was hammering right now…

He took the milk and cake and perched on a stool, trying to keep his thoughts cool. This was not why he'd decided to move to Dallas. It was about his child. About choosing not to be a long-distance father. About putting childish things away and looking after his family.

And that's when it hit him.

Lizzie *was* his family now. They would forever be tied—on holidays, over parent-teacher interviews, with dating advice, weddings, the birth of grandchildren. She would always be a part of his life.

"Why are you looking at me like that?" she asked, and he shook his head.

"Nothing. I guess I'm just a little tired."

She frowned. "Sorry if I kept you from getting back ho…I mean, back to the motel."

"No, it's good." He made a show of taking a bite of the creamy tiramisu followed by a big gulp of icy-cold milk. "It's just been a bit crazy lately. I'm kind of wondering when I'm going to get off the merry-go-round."

"Tell me about it," she grumbled, leaning her elbows on the counter and dipping into her own dessert. "I thought, with being on the board and all, that I knew what I was getting into by stepping into Dad's shoes. Turns out they're very big shoes to fill."

Chris tried to ignore the way the V of her dress gaped just a little as she leaned over, revealing a delicious glimpse of cleavage. "Do you regret taking it on, then?"

She shook her head. "No. I still believe it should be a Baron at the helm. It would help if Dad would even listen to any of my ideas. But boy, he's set in stone." She blew out a breath, took a drink of milk and scraped a bit of mascarpone onto her fork.

"What sort of ideas?" This line of conversation was slightly more comfortable, and he dropped his shoulders, trying to relax.

"Diversification, for one. I'd love for Baron to start exploring alternate forms of energy, you know? And I know Jacob agrees. But Dad's old-school oil all the way. It's maddening. I tried to get him to see it from the Roughneck point of view." She pierced the cake with her fork again. "We have the rodeo business and the stock. Then we have the farm part of it, which feeds into Savannah's store—all moneymakers. And then we have Baron Energies. He kept saying that I'm just acting like the rest of the younger generation, with my idealist head in the clouds. And then I got mad and said that people with their heads in the clouds were innovators and maybe it would do him good to spend some time up there."

Chris snorted. "And how did that go over?"

She looked up and a reluctant smile tugged at her lips. "He smacked his crutches on the patio floor, glared at me and said just how the hell was he supposed to get up there when he could barely get out of his chair?"

"Ouch."

"Quite."

"So what kind of alternate forms of energy were you thinking? Ethanol? Solar?"

"There's been great success with converting livestock

manure to gas. Several ranches I can list right now run their operations independent of the grid. Not to mention new technologies in solar cells and wind power…you'd know something about that."

"Yes, I would."

"Maybe you could talk to my dad."

He polished off his cake and added blandly, "Would that be before or after I tell him I got his eldest daughter knocked up?"

She grinned. "Good point." As she collected their plates, she kept talking. "Anyway, Dad's thing is that if we expand into other forms of energy, it's like saying we don't have faith in the oil business anymore."

"And what do you say to that?"

She met his gaze. "I told him that someone needs to start thinking about the future."

She had balls. He had no doubt about that. And he agreed with her, too. He grabbed a memory of talking to Nicole about the job and how she'd asked about Baron and mentioned Lizzie's views. "Have you been vocal about that before?"

She shrugged. "I've mentioned it a few times, but not since Dad got hurt. For now at least we don't need any more ammunition for stock prices to drop."

She put the dishes in the sink and turned around, giving a stretch. When she lowered her arms, they automatically went to her tummy and Chris's gaze followed along. "Can you feel anything yet?" he asked softly. "It's probably too early, isn't it?"

"Not yet. Probably not until I'm sixteen, seventeen weeks. I'm kind of looking forward to it. Sometimes it doesn't seem like it's even real. And then it does, because I know he or she is in there."

Chris got up from the bar stool and went into the kitchen. "I know this is kind of forward…"

She lifted her eyes, questioning.

He lifted his hand, moved it slowly towards her belly, giving her lots of time to refuse. But she didn't. She saw where his hand was going and stood very still until he pressed his wide palm against the warmth of her stomach. It was firm, but she was slim enough that he could feel the slight bubble there and his heart did something strange. "He's in there. Or she. What do you think it is?"

He wished he could feel movement but he supposed that would come later and he hoped that by that point they would still be open enough that she'd let him feel that, too.

"I don't know. I've been referring to it as she. But I noticed today you said both at different times. What do you think?"

"I said that?" He didn't remember doing that, and he left his hand against her middle. It felt good there. Good to have the connection…

"You did. I suppose all guys want a son, though, don't they?"

Did he? He supposed he did. He could picture ball gloves and bats, tools in the garage, horseback riding out at his parents' place.…

But he could just as easily picture that ball player having a ponytail and the whisper of Lizzie's freckles on the crests of her cheeks, holding out a wrench while he fixed something, or riding one of the quarter horses with ease.

"I don't think it'll matter one bit, as long as it's healthy and happy."

"Me, too."

And still his hand rested against her, their voices fell silent and the air in the kitchen hummed around them.

"I can't stop thinking about you," he admitted, his voice barely above a whisper. "I don't know why."

"Because you've had to turn your life upside down?" she suggested shakily, but he shook his head.

"I thought about you even before you showed up. Wishing I knew how to find you."

"Christopher…" It was a warning, but the long version of his name told him that she was nervous.

She slid out from his touch and skirted around him, making her way out of the kitchen to the living room. "It's late," she suggested, her eyes wide. "I have to be up early in the morning."

"And you need your rest. Of course." He offered a knowing smile and grabbed his jacket off the back of the chair. She was scared and off balance and he understood completely. Didn't mean he agreed. She wanted to take their relationship and make sure it checked certain boxes and stayed there. He wanted to see where it would lead. If it was nowhere, they'd figure that out before the baby came. But if it was somewhere, they should know that ahead of time, too.

"Thanks for dinner."

"Thanks for including me in the appointment. It was pretty special."

"I can't wait for the ultrasound," she confessed, smiling. "Pictures, not just sound."

"Can I come to that, too?"

"Of course you can."

Damn it, but why did she have to look so beautiful, so…natural? There wasn't a bit of artifice about her. Sure, she could be cool sometimes, and a bit remote. But there was not an artificial bone in her body. He liked that about her. Liked it almost as much as he liked thawing that icy demeanor that he understood she wore like armor.

He took a few steps toward her, saw her pupils widen more and dropped his jacket on the floor. Two more steps and he'd gathered her up in his arms. His mouth crashed down on hers and after the first millisecond of surprise, she responded.

Lips, tongues, teeth, hands. All were busy as Chris held her firmly against his body. This was the woman he remembered. Alive, vibrant. On fire. She made a sound against his lips and his body kicked into overdrive. It wouldn't take much to prompt him to sweep her into his arms and carry her to the bedroom.

There was a perfectly good couch and so instead he shifted his weight, nudging her backwards until they were at the edge. Another shift and his arm was braced on the back of the couch, pushing her down into the cushions. Her mouth left his and she stared up at him, her eyes shocked and aroused and her lips swollen from kissing. "Christopher," she whispered uncertainly.

"Shh," he responded, and he braced himself above her, feeling her long, lissome body beneath his. "I can't stop thinking about you. What it was like that night. How you felt in my arms. I can't pretend it doesn't exist, Liz." He slid his mouth down the column of her neck and was gratified when she gasped in response. His hips marked her, once, twice, and she pushed up against him.

He was half on top of her, half on the sofa now and it freed up one hand. He skimmed it down the soft fabric of her dress, felt the hard pebbled tip of her nipple against his palm. He slipped his fingers inside the black jersey, encountering a satin-and-lace bra that only made his pulse beat harder. Caught up in the moment, he unfastened the front clasp and tasted the sweet skin of her breast as her body jerked and thrust up to meet him.

And then her hands were pushing against his shoulders and she squirmed against him. "Stop," she commanded hoarsely. "Oh, Chris, we've got to stop."

He froze.

"What's wrong?" He looked down into her face. Was it the baby? Was she uncomfortable, did something happen? He had no experience with pregnant women, though he was pretty sure it was okay to make love during the pregnancy.

"It's just… It's too fast." Her skin was flushed and her breathing heavy. "I can't… I'm not ready… I know it sounds stupid considering…"

The phrases came one on top of the other. "Considering we already went fast?" he asked, trying to steady his breathing.

"Yeah. That." She moved one arm awkwardly, grabbing at the fabric of her dress to conceal her revealed breast.

He gazed down into her eyes, trying to isolate his brain from his body, which considering the way he was feeling at the moment, was a monumental challenge. "I want you," he stated, his voice low. "I wanted you that first night. And even if you weren't having my baby, I'd want you now. You should know that."

Her body trembled, pinned beneath his.

"But I am having your baby. And I…I need to be very, very sure this is what I want. There are no take-backs."

He closed his eyes and forced himself to inhale deeply once, twice, three times. When he opened them again she was staring up at him, her hair down and spread over the sofa cushion, so similar to that night in the motel room that he had to grit his teeth to keep from kissing her again.

"I'm sorry," she murmured.

He sighed. "Don't apologize. If you're not sure, you're not sure. That's all. Me?" He raised an eyebrow at her and tried a smile. "I'm very sure."

To his surprise she treated him to a saucy smile in return. "I can tell."

Damned if he didn't feel himself blush.

He pushed himself off her and sat back on the sofa, running his hand over his hair. "I suppose I should go then."

"Probably." Despite being the one to call a halt to their bit of fun, she sounded disappointed.

"You gonna be okay?" he asked.

She nodded.

He put his hands on his knees, preparing to push himself up when she put her hand on his thigh. "Chris? This is going to sound really strange…and I haven't changed my mind…but would you mind kissing me again? Nice and slow? It was so good before."

Hell, did she realize what she was asking? Her request went straight to his heart. It must have taken a lot for her to ask that. And the sweet yearning in her voice made him wonder if she had been missing out on romance for too long. All work and no play…

He leaned over, moving his upper body only, and met her gaze when their lips were only separated by maybe two inches. He hovered there for a moment, staring into the depths, letting her know that in this moment he was 100 percent involved.

Then, and only then, did he kiss her again, pushing down the urgency pulsing through his veins, taking his sweet time nibbling her lips, kissing the corner of her mouth as her lips dropped open and her breath came out in a jagged rush.

"God, you're good at that."

He smiled against her lips. "So are you, darlin'."

And still he kept his hands to his sides, his body planted firmly on the sofa, holding tight to the thin cord of restraint he possessed.

She was so sweet. Sweet and way more innocent than he would have expected. The girl from the motel, the girl from five minutes ago beneath him on the sofa, intoxicated his mind and body. But this girl…this girl had the ability to wrap herself around his heart.

He pushed back, rested his forehead against hers. "I can't," he said, shaken. "I can't go on and keep my promise not to touch you. Unless you've changed your mind…"

She shook her head slightly, but enough that he understood her denial.

"Then I should go. But, Liz?"

She leaned back and looked into his eyes.

"I don't want to go. You should know that, too. And decide what you want from me."

He got up, pressed a kiss to her hair, and picked up his jacket on his way to the door.

"Chris?"

He turned, his hand on the doorknob, and found her standing beside the sofa, her hair mussed, her dress twisted, and looking just about as beautiful as he could stand.

"You need to decide what you want from me, too. Because I'm not really interested in being your baby mama with benefits."

The words struck him with uncanny accuracy. He

opened the door and stepped outside into the hall. He shut it behind him without looking back, more confused than ever.

Chapter Nine

Lizzie didn't see Chris for the rest of the week. She worked long hours and tried to get as much downtime as possible. She took to calling her dad before she left the office to give him his daily update, went into the office on Saturday to stay on top of things without the usual daily interruptions, and spent Sunday cleaning her condo and doing laundry. By 8:00 p.m. she was exhausted and fell into bed and a long, deep sleep.

The only contact she'd had with Chris was a text message he'd sent, giving her the local AB Windpower office number in case she needed to reach him and he didn't answer his cell. She missed his previous chatty messages more than she cared to admit.

Maybe he was still thinking. Or maybe he'd decided it wasn't worth pursuing anything romantic with her. It would probably be easier this way. Definitely less stressful. So why wasn't she feeling more relieved?

By Wednesday her morning sickness was starting to ease up, with less vomiting and more or less just nausea until she had time for her breakfast to settle. Now she was just hungry all the time, and with the spring weather turning even warmer, she'd started wearing dresses to work that weren't so fitted in the waist. Still, she was ever aware that the time was coming that she'd have to say something to her family. She'd been running Baron for nearly three weeks now; she was almost done her first trimester. Nothing devastating had happened to the company under her management, even if her father was a stubborn old coot who plagued her for updates what felt like every hour.

The decision about when to share the news was practically made for her when Julieta left the PR department to stop by her office with an invitation.

"Okay, kiddo, you can't bury yourself in here forever. You haven't been out to the ranch in ages. We're having a family dinner this Sunday and you're coming."

Lizzie looked up at Julieta, admiring her cream-colored pantsuit and the pink scarf she'd twined around her neck. With her Hispanic complexion, the colors were stunning. It wasn't much wonder Brock had been taken with her, and little Alex, too.

"What's the occasion?" She pushed aside her calendar for a moment and gave Julieta her full attention. She didn't think it was anyone's birthday this weekend....

"Family dinner is the occasion," Julieta replied, a little sharply. "Everyone seems to be scattered everywhere these days. We haven't all been together since your dad came home from the hospital."

Lizzie smiled a little to herself. "Is he driving you crazy?"

Julieta sank down into a chair. "God, yes."

"He doesn't like to be idle."

"If he could pace while waiting for your call each day, he would. I love the video conference meetings because I know that for at least an hour he won't be irritating me about something."

"You could come back to work full-time instead of trying to do it from home. I'm sure nursing staff would look after him just fine. It's got to be killer trying to do everything and only being in the office two days a week."

"Have you ever known your dad to take to being 'looked after'? It's all I can do to get him to stay off his feet. The physiotherapist has started coming in, thankfully. By the time he finishes with that, he's ready for a nap. Don't get me wrong, I love your father and I'm happy to be home and caring for him." Her face softened a little. "I just needed to vent."

At times over the past few years Lizzie had wondered about Julieta's relationship with Brock. The age difference was so great, and even though she liked Julieta she'd wondered why she'd married a man so much her senior. And she'd wondered if at this point Brock had just been after a trophy wife.

But it was clear to her there was real affection between her dad and stepmother. "I know what you mean. He's not even in the office and he drives me crazy most days. He second-guesses everything I do and then we end up going with it anyway. But he doesn't make it easy."

"He wants to be part of the process. He still needs to be needed."

Lizzie softened a little, too. "I know that. Anyway, I should be able to make it for dinner."

"What about this Chris guy? You still a thing? He's welcome to come, too, if he's in town."

Lizzie picked up a pen and turned it over in her hands. A family dinner would probably be the perfect time for her to drop the p-bomb. "Actually, uh, he's working in Dallas right now. His company offered him management of their local office."

Julieta smiled brightly. "That's good news, right? But wasn't he competing? What happened?"

How much could she tell and still have it make sense

on Sunday? "He was, but I think the management offer was too good for him to pass up, so he cut his season short."

"Oh, well. Bring him along. I know the boys will like having him around, and Alex will be in heaven. Chris was really great to him at the hospital."

Yes, he had been. And he'd been great about a lot of things since. Great about everything except calling her over the past eight days. And that was mostly her fault.

"I'm sorry, Jul, but I've got to get to an HR meeting," Lizzie apologized. "Four-ish on Sunday?"

"Or earlier. Maybe you and Chris would like to go out for a ride. You could show him the ranch."

"We'll see."

Julieta got up and leaned over the desk to give Lizzie a hug. "Good. Now I just have to ask Savannah if she'll do dessert. No one makes pastry like that girl."

"See you Sunday. And don't let the old guy push your buttons."

Julieta laughed, a musical tinkle that made Lizzie smile. "Right back at you," she directed, then headed out of Lizzie's office.

Lizzie picked up her files and her purse and began to make her way to the boardroom. Once her meeting was done she'd have to break down and call Chris.

They'd have to talk and decide how she was going to tell the family—which included telling Brock he was about to become a grandfather.

She just hoped he had his shotgun locked away.

Lizzie picked Chris up at his motel on Sunday afternoon. She had mixed feelings about his coming to the dinner. She'd thought it would be better to tell the family alone. It would spare Chris having to answer some awkward questions and, well, she could control the outcome a bit better. But he'd insisted. Their relationship status confusion aside, he'd made the argument that if he wasn't along it would look as though he were a coward—which he wasn't. And he thought she needed backup. They were in this together.

Lizzie pulled into the lot, frowning as she put her car in park. She'd given up some control of the situation but had gained moral support. The really annoying thing was she was glad she wasn't going to have to face them down solo. Not that long ago Daniel had called her Little Miss Perfect. Not that he'd been malicious about it, but she still felt as if she were about to take a tumble off an invisible pedestal.

Chris came out of his room and pocketed his room key, still an actual key rather than the more modern key card. The motel wasn't exactly a dive, but it wasn't a four- or even three-star establishment either. He got in the passenger side and shut the door. "Hey," he said simply, settling into the seat and reaching for his seat belt. As if nothing had happened between them. As if she hadn't been sprawled beneath him on the sofa, and he'd never called her bluff.

"You haven't found a place yet?" she asked, turning out of the motel onto the street. It would take the better part of an hour to get to Roughneck, by the time she got out of this part of the city and headed east to the ranch.

He shrugged. "I'm taking my time. I don't want to have to move again, so I want to make sure I end up in a nice neighborhood. Maybe with a yard. Somewhere… safe."

For their child. He didn't need to say it for her to know that was what he meant.

"Can we make a stop on the way?" he asked. "There must be a flower shop somewhere."

"A flower shop?"

He turned his head and looked at her. "Yeah. I'd like to take something to your stepmother."

It was a sweet gesture. Lizzie gave a short laugh, though. "It's so hard to think of her that way. There's only a decade between us."

"But you get along?"

"Well enough. Not really mother-daughter."

He nodded, sitting back against the seat and relaxing. "Were you close to Brock's second wife? What was her name?"

"Peggy?" Lizzie's heart still ached when she thought of the woman who'd come into their lives at such a crucial time. "Yeah, I guess I was. I mean, I never called her Mom or anything. But she was definitely a parent. She and Dad never wavered on the rules, and she was pretty kind and understanding but tough when she needed to be."

"But she wasn't your real mom."

The ache intensified. "No."

"You've never had contact with her since she left? You have no idea where she is?"

Her jaw hardened. "No, no contact."

There was silence for a while. "Have you considered trying to find her, Lizzie?"

Her chest squeezed and she was quiet again. Eventually she answered his question. "I've considered it. Lots of times. But the truth is, she walked and never looked back. I'm not sure what good would come of looking now."

"Maybe she left it so long she didn't know how."

She turned a burning gaze on him. "That'd be a cowardly excuse now, wouldn't it? You gave up something you loved and moved across the state for a child who isn't even born yet." She looked back at the road. "I don't care about the reason. I can't imagine leaving children behind. What kind of mother does that?"

He didn't have an answer so he let the matter drop. The truth was she'd been thinking about her mother more and more since finding out she was pregnant. And the more she thought the less she understood. She already loved the baby inside her and she hadn't even planned it and the situation was less than ideal. It didn't stop the love, though.

She spotted a flower store so she pulled in and waited while he popped in for a bouquet. After that they let the radio do the talking for them as they left the city behind for the wide-open spaces of fertile ranch land. It was the second week of April; the bluebonnets had peaked the week before and spread in a stunning blue carpet along the roadsides. Lizzie loved wildflower season. When she was a girl she used to love wandering the ranch and picking blooms to bring home. No matter the weed or flower, they'd always found a place on the kitchen table. Even in the grandeur of the Baron house, the family wasn't too proud for Texas wildflowers.

"It's beautiful, isn't it?" Chris spoke softly, reaching over and turning down the radio.

"That particular shade of blue is my favorite color. Deep and dark, not quite blue and not quite purple."

"My mama used to pick them and put them on the kitchen table," he said, staring out the window, not knowing how her thoughts had taken the same direction just moments before.

"Your mom sounds great," Lizzie said weakly.

"She is. You'll like her, I think. She has a real knack for keeping things organized and on track."

"Are you calling me bossy, Christopher?"

He rewarded her with a saucy grin. "Yes. And that's not necessarily a bad thing. My mom kept everyone on schedule, dressed, fed and under budget as often as was humanly possible. She helped with my homework and expected good grades just as much if not more than my dad expected good rodeo scores." She could feel his gaze on her face. "They taught me the value of hard work and responsibility and I'll always be grateful for that."

She turned troubled eyes to his. "Are they going to hate me?"

He shook his head. "No. Not at all. I promise."

Lizzie exited off the highway and her nerves increased. "Let me tell my family, will you? When the time is right?"

He reached over and touched her thigh. "Of course. Lizzie, about the other night…"

"Don't worry about it."

"That wasn't what I was going to say. But I don't think you're ready to hear it yet. Later. Let's deal with this first. Just remember, I've got your back."

It was more than she deserved and she knew it.

"Why are you so nice to me?"

His low chuckle rode over her nerve endings. "Maybe because I don't see a reason not to be. I like you, Lizzie. I have from the start. We're in a hell of a situation but you're handling it the best you can. You've been fair and I'm trying to be fair in return. Not a bad start to parenting, really." He smiled at her, encouraging.

"You gave up your home. You moved here. You gave up your year off. And I've sacrificed nothing."

Again he laughed. "You will."

She didn't understand what he meant, but they'd reached the lane leading into Roughneck and she shuddered in a breath. "This is it," she breathed, slowing to keep the dust down as she approached the main house.

CHRIS TRIED TO keep his mouth from dropping open. He'd never been to Roughneck but he'd heard it was grand. What he'd heard hadn't done it justice. The house itself was constructed of stone, roof peaks jutting up from the manor-type design that spread across a gorgeous, green-carpeted front lawn. Several cars sat in a parking area to the left; beyond that were barns and outbuildings and fenced-in pastures where healthy-looking horses were grazing in the spring sunshine. "Holy shit," he breathed, overwhelmed. "This is where you grew up?"

She nodded. "The house wasn't always this big. When the oil strike happened, it changed everything."

It certainly had. He wasn't sure he'd been in anything this awesome in his life.

She parked next to a little car which she said was Julieta's. "Are you sure you're ready for this? My family can be a little intimidating."

"We've met, remember?"

"Yes, but my dad was unconscious. That changes a lot."

Great. Like he wasn't already nervous enough. He knew what showing up to a family dinner meant. It meant she was still up to carrying on the facade that they were a couple. Putting the best image on this as she possibly could. Trouble was, he was starting to wish it were true.

Well, he'd play along. With pleasure. For now.

"I'll be fine. I'm tougher than I look."

She laughed a little. "I hope so."

He carried his flowers loosely in his hand, following

her up the path to the front door. She didn't knock but walked right in, calling out "We're here!" in a singsongy voice. He watched as she strode ahead of him, dressed in a pretty floral sundress and sandals that were far removed from both her work attire and the sexy black dress she'd worn on their dinner date. He thought he liked this look best of all. She looked cute. Approachable.

"About time you got here!" Savannah's voice came from the kitchen and she barreled around the corner, grinning from ear to ear and capturing Lizzie in a hug. "Pecan pie. I hope you're ready for it." She stepped back and Lizzie wiped a smudge of flour off her dress.

"Chris, you made it! Good to see you," Savannah greeted, and he got the feeling that he'd have at least one ally here tonight. He was going to need it. The gorgeous stone work of the house was amazing, and above his head broad beams crisscrossed the ceiling. He didn't often feel out of his league, but he did now.

"Lizzie!" Julieta came through the French doors leading to the patio. "And Christopher. It's good to see you again."

"Good to see you, too, Mrs. Baron," he replied, handing out the flowers.

"Oh, goodness. You can't call me Mrs. Baron, it makes me feel old. Julieta is fine." She peered into the brown paper and smiled. "And these are beautiful. I'll put them in water and they'll go on our table tonight."

Julieta and Savannah both disappeared and Lizzie smiled at him. "Two down. Six to go."

"Six?"

"Dad, Carly, the boys…and Anna, our housekeeper."

Of course. A housekeeper. Why not? "Ah yes. The black-eyed-pea woman."

She flashed him a smile and then led him through the

French doors to the backyard, which was just as stunning as the interior. Cobbled stonework, glass-topped patio tables with umbrellas and comfortable chairs dotted the area around an outdoor kitchen featuring a grill the size of his motel-room bed. Fragrant smoke snuck out from beneath the grill cover while Jet reached for a set of tongs. Daniel and Jacob stood nearby, each with a beer in his hand while the patriarch of them all, Brock, sat in a wheelchair with a highball glass tipped to his mouth. Carly was nowhere to be found, and neither was Anna. A splash from his right told him that Alex was in the pool.

"Dad," Lizzie called out, reaching back and squeezing Chris's hand. She was nervous, he realized, and he squeezed back.

"Lizzie! About time you paid a visit. These phone calls and video things are way too impersonal. I've been meaning to talk to you about…"

"Not tonight, Daddy," she chided, going over and kissing his cheek. "Let's leave business for one night and just have some family time, okay?"

He frowned but nodded. "You've brought company."

She pasted on a smile and Chris followed suit. "Chris Miller, sir," he said, holding out his hand. "It's good to meet you."

Brock's strength clearly hadn't suffered from his trip to the hospital. His grip was firm and, Chris thought, issued a silent warning as they shook hands. Chris met his gaze steadily.

That's my daughter you're fooling with.

I'm not the fooling type. Sir.

Brock gave a short nod and released his hand. "Julieta tells me you were at the hospital after my accident."

"Yes, sir. Liz was upset and I went along for support."

"She said you were good to her boy. You like children, son?"

Lizzie coughed beside him but Chris never flinched. "Actually, yes, I do."

"Have any of your own running around?"

"Dad!" Lizzie protested, but Chris chuckled at the same time as Jacob and Daniel burst out laughing at their dad giving Chris the third degree.

"It's okay, Liz. I'm just getting the dad test. And no, sir, I don't have any children. Yet."

Brock smiled then, a sly grin that curved his lips just a little but lit his eyes. "You'll do. For now." He raised an eyebrow that told Chris he'd better not put a hair out of line.

Boy, was the old guy going to flip his lid when they made their announcement later.

"Chris! Chris! Watch me!"

The call came from the pool and he looked up to see Alex do a perfect cannonball from the diving board. He recognized Carly, sitting beside the pool talking to an older lady—Anna, he supposed, as she was the only one he didn't recognize.

"I think I'm being called on to judge. Excuse me?"

"Sure. You want a drink? I'll bring you one."

"Whatever you're having." He smiled at her, and then for good measure leaned over and kissed her cheek. The blush was already infusing her skin before he turned away to go to the pool.

He spent ten minutes watching Alex, until Anna told the boy he had to get out and change for dinner. Lizzie brought him a sweet tea and he chatted with Carly, who he learned was particularly interested in bull riding, and then hung with the boys, who were arguing over the ribs and making plans to fly to California the next weekend for a round-up. It was loud and boisterous and mostly good-natured—the sort of family gathering he'd missed growing up. He knew Lizzie grumbled about her family a lot, but did she realize how lucky she was?

Their child would be born into this. It was pretty incredible, but Chris couldn't help feeling like an odd man out. Like he was on the outside, looking in. Nearly a part of it but not quite.

Lizzie slid up beside him and put her arm through his. "You okay? The Barons *en masse* can be a little intimidating."

"I'm holding my own, darlin'." He smiled down at her and her gaze skittered away. "Don't be shy," he whispered, leaning his head down just a little. To anyone looking on, it would look like they were having an intimate few moments.

"I'm nervous."

"Don't be. They're your family. They love you."

"Ha! Sure they do. But they're also opinionated, judgmental, nosy..."

"Just like families are supposed to be. Relax." He should take his own advice. The thought of eight sets of eyes staring at him like a criminal who'd stolen Lizzie's virtue didn't sit well.

"How can you be so calm?" She looked up at him and he saw the nervousness in her eyes.

"Because one of us has to be," he replied, smiling.

Jet called out that the ribs were done to perfection, and bowls started appearing in a staggering number. Salads, baked beans, mounds of corn bread... The Barons didn't mess around when it came to a family dinner. There were napkins for saucy fingers and bone bowls for rib scraps.

"Come on, everyone, dig in!" Julieta called out as Jet loaded the ribs onto a huge tray.

Anna got Alex situated with his favorites and cut his ribs for him, leaving the meat on the bone so he wouldn't miss out on the messy pleasure of eating them. Chris grabbed a plate and served himself buffet style like everyone else, taking a seat beside Lizzie around the huge table.

As Alex looked up with sauce smeared on his happy face, Chris had the disturbing thought that he could get used to this. But maybe he shouldn't. This wasn't his family. And when he and Lizzie coparented, he'd still be the guy left just a little on the outside.

Chapter Ten

The noise around the table was no different from any other Sunday, but tonight Lizzie listened more carefully, speaking when she was spoken to but for the most part, keeping quiet. Brock was his regular blustery self, complaining about his wheelchair while Julieta assured him calmly that he could use his crutches when he got inside where the floor was even, so he wouldn't snub them up on the cobblestones. Lizzie's siblings razzed each other as brothers and sisters do, then moved on to talking about rodeo standings and particular events. Carly shared a story about a current female bull rider that earned her a disapproving look from her father and teasing from the boys, who all insisted the girls should stick to barrel racing and chili cook-offs—which in turn earned them well-aimed elbows from both Carly and Savannah. One big, raucous, loving family.

Now and again Chris added to the conversation, talking about past events and different horses he'd ridden—those he'd been bucked off and the ones he'd shown who was boss.

He fit in incredibly well. Too well. She certainly wasn't comfortable with it since she didn't even know her own feelings.

"You're being awfully quiet, Lizzie," Carly observed,

pushing away her plate. Tonight Carly's standard braid was done as a fishtail, making her look even younger than usual.

"Not like I could get a word in edgewise," she joked back, but she felt Chris's eyes on her to the right and she turned her head and met his questioning glance.

Is now the right time?

As right as it's gonna be.

He squeezed her hand, his lips curved the tiniest bit and she took a big breath.

"Actually, I kind of have an announcement to make."

The conversation died off and all eyes turned on her expectantly. Brock's gaze sharpened and Savannah innocently asked, "Does it have something to do with the office? You've done a great job, hasn't she, Dad?"

Lizzie swallowed and hurried to correct her. "No, not that, but thanks. I appreciate the vote of confidence." She squeezed Chris's hand back, gripping tight. "Actually, *we* have an announcement. Um…it looks like there'll be the pitter-patter of little feet around here about the middle of October."

Utter and complete silence greeted her announcement. Her own smile felt false and every single family member was staring at her with their mouths hanging open. All except Alex, who was still gnawing on his last piece of rib, unconcerned with the grown-up conversation.

"You're…pregnant?" Carly asked, her voice incredulous.

"Yeah." Lizzie's smile wavered. "I'm almost done my first trimester. Just another week or so to go." She looked over at Chris, needing the solidarity. "We actually heard the heartbeat a while back. It was pretty cool."

"Most amazing moment of my life," Chris said beside

her, and her heart nearly wept with gratitude. At least they were showing a unified front.

"Wow, talk about a shock," Jet said, the tone of his voice saying he'd never be caught dead in such a situation. Settling down was definitely not on her little brother's agenda.

"You sure know how to keep a secret," Savannah added.

Daniel elbowed Jacob. "I'll bet you fifty bucks it's a boy."

"I'll take that bet, fifty on the girl." The brothers shook hands.

Julieta's soft voice cut in smoothly. "And you're feeling all right, Lizzie? Looking after yourself?"

Chris's arm circled the back of her chair. "I'm making sure she does."

Lizzie's cheeks warmed. "Other than a bit of morning sickness, I'm fine. And hopefully that's just about over."

Still there'd been no word from Brock, and those were the words she was dreading most.

"You knew when I had my accident?"

Brock's voice was deceptively calm at the end of the table, a tone they'd all come to dread. It usually meant that either a storm was coming, or a speech that had something to do with disappointment. Lizzie wondered if she was teed up for both.

"I'd known for a week or so, yeah." She looked around the table. "That was why I was in San Antonio. I was at Chris's place, telling him the news."

And he'd only known her as Elizabeth at that point. Not that the family needed to know that. They were shocked enough about the pregnancy. They didn't need to know the sordid conception details.

"You knew when you came to me about letting you

take over at the office, and you didn't say anything about it."

"I was more worried about you. You'd been through a lot."

His fist banged down on the table. "Damn it, Lizzie. You assured me you were more than capable of handling things!"

Julieta put a calming hand on his arm. "Honey, she's pregnant, not an invalid."

Lizzie's temper bubbled. "I *am* capable of handling things! Is there anything I've done that's jeopardized the business in any way? Don't bother replying, we both know the answer is no because I report to you every night since you don't trust me enough to let me do the job on my own."

Alex stopped gnawing on his bone and looked up. Lizzie's five siblings all sat back a little in their chairs, a unanimous expression of "whoa" written all over their faces.

"Liz," Chris said quietly at her side.

"Her name is Lizzie," Brock snapped.

She saw Chris's jaw tighten.

"My name is Elizabeth," she said quietly, but with an underlying note of steel. "And Chris can call me Liz if he wants to."

"Sir," Chris began cautiously, "we wanted to tell the family all together. We're really quite excited about the baby. We hoped Lizzie's family would be, too." She noticed he'd switched back to Lizzie—a placating gesture?

"Does that mean you're getting married?" Savannah asked, and Lizzie wanted to throttle her well-intentioned sister.

"We're taking our time to figure everything out," Chris replied, cutting Lizzie off before she could answer.

Donna Alward 129

"Chris quit the circuit and took a management job with his previous company right here in Dallas, to be closer to...to us." She looked over and offered Chris a small smile. "It was a pretty big step, and we're just taking things one day at a time for now."

Brock continued to glare down the table but the family seemed to be recovering from the shock fairly well. "Well," Jet said, leaning his chair back on two legs. "I'm going to be an uncle. How 'bout that."

"It'll be nice to have a baby around again," Julieta offered gently. "I've missed that since Alex started school."

"We should have pie to celebrate," Savannah piped up. "I'll be right back."

"I'll help," Jacob offered, getting up from the table.

Carly stood, too. "Come on, Daniel, let's start clearing these dirty dishes."

"I'll help," Chris offered, getting up and taking Lizzie's and his plates and a big bowl of denuded bones.

No one thought it odd that Anna, the housekeeper and cook, didn't get up to help. She had her hands full getting Alex to the bathtub without smearing sauce on any other surfaces than his face. Lizzie smiled as she watched the older woman marshal her young charge inside. Anna had been with the family for a long time. Even when they were kids, though, they'd had to pitch in and help. Just because they'd had money didn't mean they'd been allowed to skip out on good, hard work.

"Daddy," Lizzie said quietly, wanting to smooth the waters, knowing the family had given her the space to do just that. "I'm sorry. I know the timing isn't great. I just... I knew you were worried about the company and frustrated at being injured and I didn't want to add to it. I promise I'm fine. And you'll be back to work long before the baby's born anyway."

His gaze softened a little and she was encouraged. "You're going to be a grandpa," she murmured, and pressed her hand to her belly.

"Lizzie." He sighed. "I just… Damn, girl. I kind of hoped you'd do things in the proper order."

She laughed. "Dad, please. I'm thirty already. I was so busy with my job and everything else that I never really made time for serious relationships. If I'd dated and then gotten married and finally got around to having kids, my eggs probably would have dried up."

Brock chuckled at last. "Can't really argue with that." He frowned. "Lizzie, why do you think I didn't want you to take over the company? I know you can do the job. But it's a big job, and it eats up your life. And before you know it you're getting old and falling off bulls and getting banged up and carted around in a stupid chair."

"Daddy," she whispered, and got up to go around the table and pull out a chair next to him. "You're not old."

"I'm no spring chicken, sweetheart."

She leaned over and kissed his cheek. "Well, duh."

He chuckled again.

"This Chris fellow. He's treating you right?"

She swallowed, thought back to how understanding and generous Chris had been since finding out the news. After the initial surprise he'd done just about everything right. Some things too right, she thought, remembering the way he'd kissed her on the sofa.

"Better than I deserve," she admitted.

"That's not possible," he said unequivocally.

Her heart melted. "Oh, Daddy, I love you."

"I love you, too. Which is why I say with all affection that if he hurts you, I'm gonna break both his legs. Even from this chair. I can do it."

She laughed, relieved that this conversation was drawing to a close and without too much blood spilled.

"Do you know if it's a boy or a girl yet?"

She shook her head, meeting her dad's gaze and smiling. "I'm thinking we'll leave it a surprise right until the end."

He patted her hand. "I'll be walking on my own long before then. I'm going pretty good on my crutches now."

"Well, don't do anything foolish. We're going to need you back at the head of the boardroom table, and don't you forget it."

As if the family sensed the coast was clear, the doors opened and they spilled through, carrying pie, ice cream, plates and a pot of coffee. Chris put down the stack of dessert plates and leaned over under the pretense of kissing her hair, the soft caress burning through her scalp, making the hairs on the back of her neck stand up.

"Everything okay?"

She looked up. "Sure is," she replied.

And then he did the last thing she expected. He leaned down an extra two inches and dropped a quick, but soft, kiss on her upturned lips.

He was taking the charade a little too far in her opinion. Her lips tingled from the kiss and she knew the rest of the family had seen it. When coffee was poured, Chris made sure she had a glass of milk to go with her pie. Her chair was a little too close and more than once during the conversations that followed, his arm rode along the back of her chair.

The light was softening when Alex burst back outside, dressed in cotton pajamas, his face scrubbed shiny and his dark curls damp against his scalp. "Chris, Anna said it was okay to ask if you'd tuck me in."

The request surprised everyone, since Chris was a

new addition to the family scene, but he pushed back his chair. "Sure, partner."

"'Night, Mama. 'Night, Dad. 'Night, everybody." Alex kissed Julieta and then Brock's cheek before holding out his hand to Chris. "Wait'll you see my room. Mama let me pick out my wallpaper and everything."

Lizzie watched as Chris took Alex's hand. "Let me guess. Cars?" He looked over his shoulder and winked at Lizzie.

"Cars? No way!" Alex's protest sounded as they went back in the house. "It's horses, of course."

Lizzie started cleaning up the dessert mess once he was gone and Brock wheeled himself up to the doors where Julieta was waiting with his crutches to help him over the step and inside. The boys said their good-nights and went their own ways, and Carly, Savannah, Lizzie and Anna finished putting the kitchen to rights. Carly would spend the night with Savannah in her space above the store, and head to her own home in Houston in the morning.

Anna was the first to pipe up about Chris. "Alex likes your Chris a lot," she observed, loading the last of the plates in the dishwasher.

"He likes children. Lucky for me, right?" She smiled. It wouldn't be much longer. She could keep this up for a little bit more and then they could go home and she would have a warm bath and decompress.

Carly wiped out a serving bowl and looked over at her sister. "You haven't been seeing each other that long, though, right?"

Here it comes, Lizzie thought. "It wasn't planned, no. And at first I was pretty panicked. But now…" She put her hands on her belly. "Now I'm used to the idea. I'm excited. I'm just worried that…"

She frowned. She'd never really talked to her sisters about their mother. She'd always felt it was her job to keep things together, to make the best of it. Not bring up the hurtful past.

"Worried about what, Lizzie?" Savannah put her hand on Lizzie's arm. "Is it Chris?"

Lizzie shook her head. "No. It's Mom. You guys were even younger than me, so I don't know how much you remember."

"You've been thinking about her a lot?"

"She left us. What if I'm like her? I'm worried maybe I won't be a good mom, you know?"

Anna had been listening keenly. Now she came over and gave Lizzie a big hug. "You will be fine, little one, because you have all of us to help you, and your young man, too. He's steady as they come, I think."

She only felt marginally better. "I wish I could talk to her and ask her why she left."

Anna's gray head bobbed in agreement. "I know." If the housekeeper had any idea of why, she'd never said. Not once over the years.

"Are you thinking of looking for her?" Carly asked, her eyes wide.

"I don't know. She's going to be a grandmother now…."

The women were all silent for a minute, pondering that idea.

"Well," Lizzie said, a little lighter, "like I said tonight, one step at a time and there's no rush, is there?" She wiped her hands on a dish towel. "Do you guys mind if I skip out for a bit? I wanted to show Chris the barns and the arena before we go. We didn't have a chance earlier."

"Go ahead. This is pretty much done anyway."

She stopped at the den to say good-night to Brock and Julieta, and then made her way to Alex's room. She peeked inside and saw Alex sitting up in bed, Chris perched on the side of the mattress, reading from a book. She stayed hidden, listening to Chris's deep voice take on the character of a cowboy who kept losing his clothes when he slept and so learned to sleep with his boots on. She smiled as he got to the end and Alex asked for one more story.

"Sorry, partner, I promised your mom just one. You need your sleep."

"Awwww!"

"Trust me, Alex. Most of the time it's in your best interest to listen to your mom."

"Dad says it's good training for marriage," Alex piped up, and Chris laughed.

"Can this cowboy stand one more kiss good-night?" Lizzie asked, stepping into the room.

"I guess. You're too old to have girl germs."

"Ouch!"

Alex grinned at Lizzie, well aware that he'd delivered a perfect insult. She ruffled his hair, and then tickled his ribs. "Good night, scamp."

"'Night, Lizzie. Are you really having a baby?"

She smiled down at him with affection. Most of the time Alex seemed like a nephew rather than a brother. "Yes, I'm really having a baby."

"Good. Now maybe Mama will quit treating me like one."

Chris stifled a laugh as Lizzie tucked in the covers. "Sweet dreams." She kissed his cheek.

Alex curled his fingers around his comforter and rested his head on the pillow. "Leave my night-light on, 'kay?"

Lizzie and Chris left the room, shutting the door but leaving it open a crack.

"Do you want to see the barns before we go? I meant to give you a tour earlier."

"That'd be nice."

"I already said my goodbyes, so we can just leave when we're done."

"If you're too tired…"

She shook her head. "No, I think some fresh air and a walk is just what I need. Come on."

They ambled through the twilight to the first of the barns. She flicked on a light and the long corridor lit up. She'd spent lots of time in here as a kid, helping clean stalls, feeding horses, polishing tack. She'd enjoyed the ranching side of the business as well as the other kids, though she'd never quite got into the rodeo scene the way they had. She'd been more into the oil side of things from the start. She'd enjoyed following her dad into the office, sitting up on a spare chair and doodling while he worked.

"Wow, this is some setup," Chris said, stepping forward. "My dad would be in heaven."

"Jet's place is down the road. He likes his independence. Still, the boys are pretty active here, especially with the arena. They do a lot of their training here."

"You keep bucking stock?"

"Yessir." They walked down the quiet corridor, their shoes echoing on the concrete floor. Chris stopped at the tack room and looked inside. "Holy cow. This is huge."

She flicked on that light, too, illuminating the long room that smelled like leather and rags and oil—memories of her childhood. "I love this room," she confessed. "When I was younger, I'd sneak down here with a book and disappear. Saddle blankets are a mighty comfortable reading bench."

"You came here a lot?"

She looked up at him with a small smile. "Are you

kidding? With two sisters and three brothers? Peace and quiet was a valuable commodity."

He laughed and ran his hand over a smooth saddle, his fingers tracing the elaborate design on the fender flap. She tried not to stare at the gentle movement of his hands, caressing the supple leather.

"We've got some new babies right now that are out with their mamas in the corral," she suggested, scrambling for conversation. "You want to see?"

He nodded, so she shut off the lights and they went back out into the corridor. At the end, she rolled back the door and led him to the white-fenced corral next to the barn.

Lizzie looked at the mares and foals differently now that she was expecting her own baby. There was no question the sight of them made her heart go a little mushy. Her hand drifted once more to her tummy, an action that was becoming rather automatic as she got used to her pregnancy. Mamas and babies—strong, solid legs and fragile, gangly ones. Stability and fragility as the unsteady foals relied on the security of their mothers. Together Lizzie and Chris rested their elbows on the top rail of the fence and watched as one soft, chestnut-colored foal with white socks nuzzled close to his mom to nurse.

"They're so adorable at this age, aren't they? All soft and fuzzy and wobbly?"

Chris nodded and gave a soft laugh. "And then they turn into teenagers and want to buck you off into oblivion."

She grinned. "Well, that's their job."

"My dad, he was foreman on a ranch where they raised working stock. I used to love it. Lived for it. I spent my weekends cleaning stalls and grooming horses when I was small, and then I got into rodeo. His boss's son and I started out as juniors together. I was lucky, because Mom and Dad probably couldn't have afforded to do that for me. Jeb Tucker treated me like I was his own kid."

"Sounds like you had a good childhood."

"The best," he confirmed. "The kind I'd like to give my child, too."

Her heart softened even more. "You're going to be a good dad, Christopher. Maybe how we met was less than ideal, but…I'm starting to think that if this had to happen, I got pretty lucky."

His shoulder nudged hers. "We're going to be all right, aren't we?" he asked.

She nodded. "I think so. I think we both want to put this baby first, and as long as we do that, everything else will fall into place."

"Liz…"

He turned to her and it felt like the most natural thing in the world to let him put his arms around her and kiss her. His lips tasted like Savannah's pecan pie and the scent of his cologne mingled with the verdant smells of springtime—grass and bluebells and rich, fertile soil. He shifted just a little, and her arms slid around his back, running over the taut muscles beneath his shirt.

"Whew," he breathed, breaking off the kiss.

She smiled shyly, though inside desire was pounding through her. Maybe it was just a hormonal surge, but his kisses lit her up like Fourth of July fireworks.

"You want to see the arena Dad built? The boys do a lot of their training there." It would probably be good to change the subject, not let anything get out of hand.

"Does it mean we'll be out of view of the house?"

There was an urgency to his voice that made her heart pound. "Maybe the arena isn't a good idea," she retracted.

"Maybe the arena is a great idea," he replied, his eyes dark with intent as twilight fell around them.

"Chris…"

"Stop analyzing everything. I'm enjoying getting to know you in your element."

"What's that supposed to mean?" She tilted her head up, frowning a little.

"It means," he murmured, leaning forward and nuzzling her ear, making her shiver with delight, "that your condo is a bit of a mystery. There's not a lot of you in it. But here, with your family…" He smiled against her cheek. "It's very illuminating."

She'd have to remember to ask him what that meant later. Right now she was having a hard time focusing on much of anything, Chris was being so distracting.

He took her hand and led her to the door of the arena, slipping inside but leaving the lights off.

Nerves bubbled around in her stomach. She should be pulling away. Should be insisting that they leave and go home. Should be protesting that this would only make things worse…

The problem was she wanted to be with him as much as he seemed to want to be with her. The attraction of that first night hadn't been a one-time, flip-it-off-with-a-switch kind of feeling. It was still there. It was in the tingling of her lips where he'd kissed her, the ache of her fingertips wanting to touch him.

"Th-this is the arena. As you can see we had chutes put in on the west side for when the boys want to train, and over there we have barrels for barrel racing." She pointed a shaky finger but Chris caught her hand and clasped it in his.

"That's all very interesting," he whispered. "Do you know that I always thought it was crazy when people spoke of a pregnant glow? But now I get it, because you have it, Lizzie. You have a light about you that is beautiful."

She'd been melting without needing the sweet words, but having them weakened her resolve even more. No one had ever called her beautiful before. Smart, efficient, driven, responsible…but not beautiful.

And sometimes a girl liked to be called pretty, she admitted, if only to herself.

"What are we doing, Chris?" He was standing too close again, and she felt her shoulders and bottom touch the smooth wall at the entrance to the ring as she stepped backward. There was nowhere to go now—not that she really wanted to.

"Getting to know each other. We're doing what we would have done if we'd met here, gone out on dates like a normal couple."

If they'd done things in the predictable order, he meant. If they hadn't hooked up and jumped instantly into bed. If there had been no consequences to their poor judgment…

Consequences.

"Stop thinking," he suggested, running a hand down her arm. "Just for a little while. Just stop and let yourself *be*."

The arena was dark and he pressed up against her, just lightly, but enough that her body came alive at every point where they touched. His lips teased hers, soft and warm as he melted against her. She could feel the hard planes of his body against her skin, through her shirt, and she lifted a hand, running it under the soft cotton and over the warmth of his taut ribs.

Holy smokes, he was firm and muscled and she felt the way his breath caught beneath her fingertips. The pressure against her mouth intensified and he shifted, moving one hand over her shoulder, down her collarbone to cup her breast in his hand. The pressure felt so good she rolled into it a little, knowing they should stop but not wanting to at all.

His hips came flush with hers and she felt the evidence of his desire.

"You still do this to me," he murmured, cradling her face in his hands, kissing her in between snatches of words. "I don't know why, or how. You kill me, Lizzie. Come home with me tonight."

"What about keeping things simple?"

He shook his head, but she could see the intense look in his eyes despite the dark shadows. "We'll never be simple, Liz. I'm starting to realize that."

He kissed her again, turning her knees to jelly. She'd always been one to keep her head about her when it came to men. Never lost sight of her goals or priorities. Why was Christopher Miller so different? Why did he seem to have special sexy powers where she was concerned?

"Not your motel room," she disagreed. "Not like before. Come to my place. Just this once. Just to…scratch this itch we can't seem to get rid of."

He didn't answer, just lifted his head enough that she could see the fire blazing in the dark depths. Then he took her hand in a firm grip and led her from the arena.

Apparently the tour was over.

Chapter Eleven

Sunlight filtered through the cracks of Lizzie's blinds and she squinted against the glare, opening one eye just a crack to check the clock beside the bed.

Seven-thirty.

She should get up. She was usually ready to leave for the office by now if she wasn't there already, getting ahead of the big rush on the DART that took her right downtown. This morning there was another warm body beside her in the bed, though, and she hadn't gotten up and snuck away like she had the first time they'd been together.

Chris lay beside her, flat on his stomach, his face turned towards her on the mattress and the sheets pooled around his hips.

He was naked under there. And damned if the idea didn't hold more allure than it should.

"Enjoying the view?" he asked, without opening his eyes and her cheeks flamed.

"How did you know I was watching you?"

His eyes were still closed but a smile crept up his cheek, popping a dimple. "Trade secret."

He opened his eyes and braced up on his elbows. "Good morning, by the way. What time is it?"

"Seven-thirty."

"Hmm. I think we're both running late."

"Seems like."

He rolled to his side and under the covers, found her hip with his fingers. He kneaded gently. "You okay?"

Sometimes he was so considerate. "Yeah, I'm okay. You?"

He grinned. "You have to ask? I've been thinking about that since the first morning when I woke up and you were gone. You can't believe my relief to find you still here this morning."

"You thought about me…that way?"

"Are you kidding?" His eyebrows went up. "Of course I did. I planned to ask you out again except you took off and I really didn't know where to find you."

His fingers continued to knead at her hip. "Liz, I'm not a one-nighter kind of guy. I'm starting to think that fate maybe had a little part in bringing us together."

What surprised her was how she wanted to believe him. Over the past few weeks she'd found herself thinking not about visitation schedules and a congenial co-parenting relationship, but what it would be like to be… closer. Wondering if they could make it work between them. She hadn't had a serious relationship since she'd started working full-time. The few dates she'd been on had been with men more interested in her last name than in her.

But Chris hadn't even known her last name. And yesterday he'd said he'd liked getting to know her better.

"So," he said, leaning in, "let me ask the question I would have asked almost three months ago. Where do we go from here?"

She blinked. "You've got to understand. I'm afraid that if we start something, and it doesn't work out, that it'll make things unbearable when the baby comes."

"Honey, I think we've passed the 'start something' stage."

She couldn't help it, her lips curved up just a little. "Ha ha. But you know what I mean, right?"

"Yeah, I know what you mean." He propped his head up on an elbow.

"You wouldn't have moved to Dallas if I hadn't gotten pregnant," she pointed out.

"I might not have stayed with AB at all," he mused. "Part of my year off was to decide what I really wanted to do. If I even wanted to be an engineer anymore."

Her heart sank. He'd made life changes for her unborn child and big changes at that. How could they possibly make it work? She could just imagine a year, two years, five years down the road. Would he blame her for him being stuck in his job? Resent her? He'd deny it now, she knew that for sure. But it was a long time to spend in a job you didn't like.

"You could still change your mind."

"Working in my current job is the best way to provide for my kid," he said simply, and she got it. It was pride. She had her own fair share and so did her father.

"Okay," she said softly. "But what about us?"

He reached out and brushed a piece of hair off her face, tucking it behind her ear. "We could take it slow. Do you think you could be open to…exploring whatever is between us?"

Open to it? She was already contemplating it. "I think I might…if we laid out some ground rules."

He smiled again, and pushed himself up into a seated position, the comforter resting loosely at his hips. "Ah, yes. The rules. Very important."

She nudged his arm, silently chastising him not to be a brat. She ticked off items on her fingers. "We take things slowly," she began. "We both reserve the right to back off at any time if it's not working. We agree to keep things friendly no matter what." She looked into his eyes. "We put our baby first in all things."

His gaze clung to hers. "I can live with all those conditions."

"You can?"

A slow smile lit his face. "Of course I can. I would have suggested the same." He looked at the comforter, which she just realized had slipped a little, revealing the rounded curve of her breast. "We might have already goofed at the going slow part, though."

"Well, it's not like we have to worry about me getting pregnant," she quipped, pulling up the comforter.

"Nope," he said softly, leaning closer. He pulled down the bedding, revealing the top half of her body and she shivered all over, both from the cold air but mostly from anticipation.

"Christopher," she warned, but the word was infused with as much desire as it was caution.

"I bet you're never late for work," he murmured, nuzzling at her neck until it was hard for her to breathe.

"Not usually," she managed to say, trying her best to stay immune.

"Today could be an exception." He smiled against her skin.

His fingers were doing mad, wonderful things under the covers and she gave up. "I could go in late one day," she relented, her head dropping back as her agenda for the day fluttered clean out of her head.

Chris chuckled, then pulled the covers up over them both.

THE WORKDAY WAS well underway when Lizzie straightened her jacket and stepped out of the elevator. For the first time, she realized she'd decorated her condo in a similar way to the offices—lots of black, chrome and white. It was professional-looking and impressive, but it didn't have a lot of personality. Even the orchid at the main reception desk was white and in a black lacquer pot. The overall feel was rich and efficient but it wasn't friendly or comfortable.

Damn Chris and his comments about her condo. Had she been so busy working that she'd unwittingly brought the office into her own home?

"Good morning, Ms. Baron," the receptionist greeted, and Lizzie smiled at her.

"Good morning." She went farther into the office, back to her office with the window overlooking the Dallas skyline. Maria, Brock's secretary, popped up from her chair as soon as Lizzie passed by her desk.

"Lizzie. It's nine-fifteen."

"Sorry I'm late." Lizzie smiled. "Are there messages?"

"Messages?" Maria's brows went up as her lips dropped open in dismay. "Lizzie, you had an eight-thirty meeting with Mark Baker."

Shit shit shit. The words ran through Lizzie's head as she halted in her tracks. "Is he still available?"

"I'll check. But he's not happy and you know what he's like."

"Looking for any opportunity," Lizzie agreed, her stomach twisting in knots.

"I tried to call you, but you didn't pick up."

She hadn't because her cell had gone dead last night and she hadn't had time to charge it before leaving for the train. "Give him a quick call and tell him I'll meet him in my office…no, in Dad's office. In ten minutes. And I'd love a cup of herbal tea."

Maria gave a crisp nod and Lizzie felt doubly bad. "Maria?"

The woman turned back and Lizzie tried a smile. "Thank you. For everything you've been doing lately. I couldn't manage this without you and Emory."

"Keep your chin up," Maria advised, her posture softening just a little. "Mark'll try to bully you. Don't let him."

Lizzie grinned. "Yes, ma'am."

She made sure she was ensconced in her father's plush leather executive chair and had taken a revivifying sip of hot tea when Mark strode into the office, looking like Mr. *GQ* in an impeccably tailored suit, not a hair on his blond head out of place.

"Sorry for the confusion, Mark. I appreciate you changing your schedule."

"Anything for the boss," he replied, taking a seat across the desk from her. "How's your dad?"

"Doing well," she replied, picking up her tea and trying to look relaxed. Mark Baker didn't like her. She knew that. It didn't help that he was the football all-star guy with the thousand-watt smile and a near-perfect GPA. She'd worked hard to find perfection and never really found it, so seeing it across the desk from her was plenty intimidating. "I had dinner out at the ranch last night. He's not used to taking a backseat for this long, but we talk every night about what's coming up. No surprises that way."

Translation: you're not just dealing with me here.

They spent twenty minutes going over the latest figures, changes to the operational budget that made her head spin, and when her eyes were starting to glaze over, he tapped his reports together, put them to the side and pulled out another file.

"I thought you should see this," he said, handing over a sheet.

She picked it from his fingers and stared down at numbers and a graph. "Our stock?" She looked up at him. "We knew it would take a hit when Dad was hurt. Yes, the stock price went down but less than we expected by a couple of percentage points."

"The press release was a good idea," he conceded. "And as much as it pains me to admit it, having someone with the last name Baron step into Brock's place was a good move."

"So what's your issue?" she asked, her stomach growling. She'd had a bowl of oatmeal and fruit that Chris had insisted she eat before leaving for the office, and already she was hungry again. With a bit of a start, she realized that this was the first morning in several weeks now that she hadn't been sick at all.

"Look at it again," he instructed.

"What am I looking for?" She felt stupid asking it. "I see that our stock price has rebounded a bit since the accident. That's good, right?"

He took the paper back and clicked on his pen, circled a spot, and handed it back.

"Trading activity?"

"Someone's buying up stock, and getting it at a pretty good price. Normally that would be a good thing, but something twigs me the wrong way about it. Considering our position right now, and the fact that after your dad's accident, people were selling off their stock…this is too big a volume to be coincidence."

"Are you sure?"

He gave her a long, cool stare. "No, I'm not sure. But it was enough of a jump to raise a red flag for me."

"Why would someone do that?"

He sighed. "Because we're vulnerable? Because they have insider information? I can't know for sure. If it's a publicly traded company, they have a while before they have to divulge their purchase to their stockholders."

She forgot about his smugness for a moment. "What are you really thinking, Mark?"

"I'm thinking someone wants a piece of Baron Energies. And they're hoping that their purchase of our stock will go unnoticed because we're not focused at the moment."

But he was focused. For all his faults, Lizzie knew one thing. Mark Baker was very, very good at his job.

"Thanks for bringing it to my attention."

"That's my job," he answered. "And I'll stay on top of it, keep running the numbers, see what I can find out. Maybe it's nothing, but I'd rather be safe than sorry."

"What can I do?" She swallowed her pride and met his gaze. "What should I do?"

He frowned. "Lizzie, you know I didn't support the idea of you sitting in the driver's seat."

"I know you don't like me…."

"It's not that at all." His blue eyes met hers directly. "This was the reason. You're great at the human resources area, a whiz with manpower. You're good with the press. You're a great face for the company—a young, successful, independent woman from a strong family. But this side of things? This isn't your strong suit and we both know it."

Ouch. His assessment stung even if she secretly believed he was correct. "That's why I'm surrounded by people who are all brilliant in their areas of expertise. That's why I trust them."

He smiled a little. "Right. I got the message."

"And I got yours, Mark. I know we're not besties or

anything, but I'd like to think we both have the best interests of Baron at heart."

"Me, too. Do you want me to talk to your father about this?"

"No." If she were going to sit in the big-girl chair, she needed to do the hard work. "I will."

"Fair enough. I'll keep you posted."

"I'll be here."

He closed his file and got up to leave. He was halfway to the door before he turned back to face her. "Lizzie?"

"Yes?" She put down her pen and looked up.

"When you turned me down before...why did you say no?"

She blinked. It was the last thing she'd expected him to ask, and she wasn't sure how to answer. In the end she figured honesty was best. "Because you were too sure of yourself. Cocky. Like you'd be doing me a favor."

He smiled, an arrogant upturning of his lips that showed perfect teeth. "So I would have," he replied, sliding one hand into his trousers pocket.

Lizzie couldn't help but grin back because she could tell now that he was teasing. "Yeah, well, there's a difference between confidence and arrogance. One's sexy. The other...not so much." She thought back to Chris and his quiet assertiveness and knew which she preferred. "But," she conceded, "you're a very good CFO for Baron so I've forgiven you for being a bit of a jerk."

He laughed then. "Sitting in the big chair has made you more sure of yourself," he observed. "Your dad better look out. You might get comfortable sitting there."

Except in just under six months she'd be going on maternity leave. "I don't think there's any worry about that."

He was just turning to leave when there was a knock

on the door. "Lizzie?" Emory poked her head in. "There's someone here to see you."

She stepped aside and Chris walked through the doorway, carrying a white paper sack and a cellophane-wrapped bouquet of daisies.

She was surprised, and pleased, too. Chris's answering smile lit up the office and Mark looked from one of them to the other. "Well. That explains a lot," he remarked, still smiling a little. He held out his hand. "Mark Baker."

Chris shifted the paper bag into his left hand with the flowers and shook Mark's hand. "Chris Miller. Nice to meet you."

"I'll let you two catch up. Lizzie—let me know how it goes with your father."

"Will do. Thanks, Mark."

Mark left and Emory shut the door behind him, leaving Chris and Lizzie alone. "I didn't expect to see you this morning."

He smiled. "I called into the office after I ran back to the motel to change. I'm actually going out in the field this afternoon, so I thought I'd play hooky for another hour and stop by. I don't want to tie you up, though, so I won't stay long."

She was stupidly pleased to see him, especially after last night. "What's in the bag?"

"Muffins. Bran blueberry with walnuts. Something healthy for the both of you."

"Are you saying I'm getting fat?" She was only teasing, but her question prompted him to move forward. He put the bag and the flowers on the desk and then put his hands on her hips.

"I'm not saying that at all. And I promise you that over the next few months, when you start showing and your curves get a little curvier…you will only be more beautiful."

"Are you one of those men who have a thing for pregnant women?"

He looked deep in her eyes. "No. Just the one who's pregnant with my baby."

If he kept this up she'd be swooning half a dozen times a day. Her stomach rumbled again and she broke the spell with a laugh. "Looks like your muffins are well-timed. Oh, hey, guess what? I wasn't sick this morning."

"I was a good distraction."

"Maybe. Maybe it's just letting up, like the doctor said it would." She turned away and reached for the bag. "Are you joining me?"

"Naw. I, um, might have had one on the drive over."

She laughed. "Couldn't wait?"

"I seem to have worked up an appetite," he answered. "Lizzie, about last night…"

Her body tingled with simple awareness. "One day at a time, remember?"

His gaze warmed and he nodded slowly. "Yeah. I know we're supposed to just take things as they come and see how it goes. I just…" She clutched the top of the bag tightly, hanging on his words. He came close, so that their bodies were only a few inches apart and her breath was coming faster. "I just wanted you to know that it was good."

There was a hesitancy in his voice that she liked. He wasn't quite sure of himself. Wasn't quite sure of them. And he definitely wasn't taking anything about them for granted.

For the first time, she felt like someone actually saw her for her. Not because of her last name or who the members of her family were or the letters after her name. But her. Liz. The person underneath all the other details that somehow formed an image that bore little resemblance to the person inside.

And that was why she'd gone with him that first night. That was why she'd walked into a bar in jeans and boots and a devil-may-care attitude.

"It was good for me, too," she murmured.

"It's a good start," he decreed. "Listen, I hate to do this, but I've got to go."

"Thanks for the flowers and the muffins. It was so thoughtful." They were barely an inch apart now.

She tilted her chin just a little, inviting him that much closer. He touched her lips with his, a gentle contact that rocked her right to the bottom of her sensible pumps. He took his time, keeping it light and yet devastatingly intimate as his hands lightly gripped her arms. When the kiss broke off, he ran his tongue over his lips once and murmured, "Mmm."

"I need to get to work, Mr. Miller, and you're proving to be a big distraction."

"Can I see you again tonight?"

So soon. It scared her and exhilarated her at the same time. "I should be home around seven. I'll make dinner."

"That sounds perfect. I'll see you then." He kissed her forehead just as Emory stuck her head in the nearly closed door once more. "Lizzie, you've got a call from legal. Can I put them through?"

Lizzie's cheeks heated as she looked over Chris's shoulder at her assistant, whose face was completely deadpan. "That'd be fine, Em. Chris was just on his way out."

"See you tonight," he said, backing away from her and turning toward the door.

She watched him leave, her heart pounding in her

chest. Who knew he'd end up being so romantic? So spontaneous?

The phone buzzed as Emory put through the call and Lizzie snapped back to reality. She had a job to do and she'd better start doing it, rather than mooning over Christopher all day.

Chapter Twelve

The next few weeks passed in a blur. Lizzie spent long hours at the office and updated Brock as needed, but kept those conversations to a minimum. She never really had time to bring up the stock issue once they were done dealing with other topics, and Brock was particularly grouchy these days since he'd caught his crutch on a rug and taken a fall. Between the pain and the physio, she tried to bother him as little as possible.

Mark hadn't brought it up again either, so she focused on crisis management for the time being and went home exhausted every night.

The good part of that was the way Chris had become a part of her life. He never pushed about the future, but she knew deep down he was becoming deeply entrenched into her day-to-day existence. After the first few nights at her place, he left a toothbrush in her bathroom and she picked up bottles of his scent of body wash and shampoo at the drugstore to keep in her shower. By the weekend he'd brought over some clothes, and by that Sunday night she'd pretty much told him it was foolish for him to be paying for a motel room when he was never there and gave him a key to her condo. He could stay with her until he found a place to live.

So far he'd found himself a Realtor and had turned

down a few properties south of the city due to their price. He was just getting started, though, and in the evenings they often spent a half hour or so looking at properties online. One in particular they both loved, and it was only minutes away from Roughneck. The ranch was small but well-kept, the house a two-story colonial with regal white columns out front. It was also about twice his budget, but each night they brought it up and looked at it just for fun. At times she fantasized about what it would be like to live in such a place *together,* but then she pushed the thoughts away. They were taking things one day at a time. Nothing serious. No commitments or big decisions.

While she was cautious about their relationship, she was much less so about motherhood. Lizzie started looking for things for the baby. One lunch hour she popped into a shop, found herself misty-eyed staring at plush teddy bears and bought two. She bought magazines to inspire the decoration of the nursery and ordered a padded rocking chair.

The chair was delivered to the condo on Thursday night and the delivery men left it in the living room until Lizzie could decide where she wanted it put. Chris came home and discovered her sitting in it, her hands on the curved arms, sinking into the soft cushions and rocking back and forth.

"New furniture?" He raised an eyebrow and smiled at her, closing the door.

"I couldn't resist. I was passing by and saw it and it was a total impulse buy."

"What? Ms. Total Planner? But what if the stain color doesn't match the crib you want?"

She laughed. "Oddly enough, I'm worrying less about stuff like that lately."

He came forward and bent down for a kiss. "Good. Less stress is good for you and the baby."

She frowned and kept rocking. "I wouldn't say I have less stress. I've been meaning to talk to my dad about something Mark brought to my attention last week and I don't quite know how to bring it up."

"Oh?" She watched as Chris moved to the kitchen and retrieved a pot, filled it with water and put it on the burner to heat.

"There's been a lot of stock activity since Dad's accident. We expected the price to dip, but there's been a lot of buying lately, too." She frowned. "You know, our position in the industry took a hit when we lost that contract in the Gulf. I can't help feeling that we might have weathered that better if we were more diversified."

Chris poured marinara into a pot to heat and began slicing chicken breasts. "You think someone's making a move on the company?"

"I don't know. Other than Mark's 'feeling' about the stock, there's no evidence."

"But you're worried."

"Of course I'm worried." She stopped rocking, looked up at him as he stood at the stove, his upper half visible through the opening above the serving counter.

He met her gaze. "You're just particularly sensitive because you're new to this and you're feeling pressure, that's all. I know you don't want to disappoint your dad."

"Not just Dad. The company, too. I love it. I always have. It's more than just an office to me."

"I know." He frowned a little.

"What?" She pushed herself up out of the chair. "You don't like me running the company?"

"If you love it, you should." He slid pasta into the now-boiling water. "I'm just, well, a bit jealous. Not everyone finds the one thing that they really love and makes a career out of it."

She felt a little guilty then, knowing he'd given up something he'd loved to be there for her and the baby. But he needn't have done that so soon. He could have finished out the season.

She went into the kitchen, paused by the refrigerator and watched as he sautéed the chicken, pushing it around with a wooden spoon. "Chris, why did you leave the rodeo behind so fast after I told you the news? I know you said you wanted to support your child, but he or she isn't even born yet."

"Because I was kidding myself," he answered bluntly. "I took a year off to play, but I knew deep down it was just a vacation. It's not real life." He smiled at her. "I found out I was going to be a father and I decided I needed to stop wishing for my youth back and start growing up."

"But are you happy? Really happy?"

He shrugged. "Is anyone ever completely and perfectly happy? I doubt it."

He came over to her and put his hands on her shoulders. "Listen. If we hadn't met, you wouldn't be expecting a baby. And if you weren't pregnant, we wouldn't be here right now. And here isn't such a bad place to be." His dimple popped and she couldn't deny him anything when he smiled like that.

No, here wasn't a bad place to be at all. But she couldn't escape the feeling that he was putting on a bit of a show just the same. That not everything was as cozy as it seemed. The problem, she realized, was that it all felt a little too good to be true. And the problem with that was in her experience, if it felt too good to be true it generally was.

"It's just a job. Don't sweat it." He brushed it off and went back to the stove to stir the meat.

She paused for a moment and then decided to let it drop. "Is there anything I can do to help?" she asked.

He smiled brightly. "Salad?"

She went to work making a green salad to go with their dinner when Chris brought up another subject. "I spoke to my parents today. I think we should tell them. How do you feel about going for a drive this weekend?"

She frowned. Things were busy at work and she'd planned to go over some operational reports away from the office. Then again, they'd told her family nearly two weeks earlier and Lizzie was feeling better. After all Chris's sacrifices, the least she could do was revise her schedule.

"That'd be fine," she replied, tossing the salad with the forks.

It was all very domestic. Very…settled. She should be happy. He was a good man, they got along well, and the sparks—well, they were there, too.

So why did she feel as if they were living in a house of cards, and the slightest interfering breeze would blow it down?

CHRIS WAS DEFINITELY aware of the differences between the Miller spread and the Baron ranch. No gated entry and grand stone mansion, no manicured lawns, modern barns or a swimming pool in the back. Just a one-story ranch-style bungalow, a neat lawn with some bedding plants livening the place and a vegetable garden off to one side. A late-model half-ton truck sat in the driveway next to a used but reliable compact car.

"You grew up here?" Lizzie asked from the passenger seat. They'd brought his truck today; his parents would expect it and he enjoyed driving it more than Lizzie's luxury car if he were being honest.

"All my life," he answered, strangely nervous. "Dad works at a neighboring ranch and my mom has a part-time job at the library in town."

It was nothing compared to her lifestyle in Dallas.

"It's nice growing up in one spot, isn't it?" She turned her bright eyes to him and smiled. "We had some insta-bility in our lives, with our mom and with Peggy dying, but we always had Dad and Roughneck. There's a lot to be said about the security of constancy."

He'd always felt so, too.

"It must have been hard for you to move. You were so close to your parents and could visit whenever you wanted."

"It's not that far to drive," he said, but she was right. He'd missed being a little closer. Checking in to make sure they were all right. His mom had had a bout of an-gina the year before and years of handling livestock had left his dad in good shape but dealing with a bit of ar-thritis in his knees.

He parked next to the car and got out right away to open Lizzie's door. She reached into the middle of the bench seat and took out a bakery box containing an or-ange chiffon cake. Lizzie had insisted on bringing des-sert and had planned on baking, she said. But in the end she'd worked late into the evening and they'd stopped at a bakery instead.

When he shut the door behind her, he turned around to find his mother on the front steps. "Christopher Miller. About time you got your sorry hide back here."

He wouldn't have expected any other greeting and his heart lightened as he smiled. "Where's Dad?"

"Just finishing up in the shower. When he heard you

were bringing a woman home with you, he decided to spruce up."

Mrs. Miller smiled at Lizzie. "We're very happy to have you here. Should I call you Liz? That's what Chris has called you."

To his relief Lizzie smiled in return. "Liz is fine. Thanks for having us over for dinner, Mrs. Miller."

"Oh, go on and call me Debra, none of this Missus business."

He was thankful she hadn't insisted on being called Mom—and also thankful for the warm welcome. His parents hadn't been totally happy about his move to Dallas, after all.

"Come in, come in," Debra invited, holding open the screen door. "I've got fried chicken ready to go on and Chris's favorite mashed potatoes. Hope you're hungry."

Lizzie smiled up at him as they crossed the threshold into the house. "Always," she whispered, and Chris laughed. It was true. She had a healthy appetite for sure.

His mother took the bakery box from Lizzie and put it on the kitchen counter after peeking beneath the lid and oohing over the cake. "Let's take a cool drink out on the back verandah," she suggested. "And we can catch up while Robert makes himself pretty."

Chris watched as Lizzie accepted iced tea from his mother and then went outside to the shaded verandah. His mom picked a comfortable padded chair and left the two-seater swing empty. He held out a hand, inviting Lizzie to sit down and then he sat beside her.

"Oh, this is lovely," Lizzie said, letting out a breath. "There's nothing like wide-open space to blow your troubles away, is there?"

Chris looked over at her, surprised at her observation. She was the kid who enjoyed the business, living in the city. And yes, she fit in at Roughneck but even that was very different from the simple life his folks led.

"How right you are," his mom agreed. "Now that it's just Bob and me, sittin' on that swing at the end of the day is just about perfect."

He watched Lizzie as she smiled and her eyes lit up with impish humor. "We had a tire swing at our house when we were little. I used to sit in it and spin around and look up at the sky. My brother thought it would be fun to spin me around and around and let me go. But it backfired."

"What happened?" Chris asked, intrigued by this side of Lizzie. She was so open. So guileless.

So much like the woman he'd met at the bar. Unencumbered.

"The ride ended, I got out of the tire and threw up on his boots," she replied, and the three of them laughed. "He never tried that again."

A slap of the screen door announced Chris's dad's arrival. He came outside dressed in clean jeans and a button-down shirt, his face freshly shaved and a glass of tea in his hand. "Sorry I'm late to the party," he greeted, pulling up a chair beside Debra. "I smelled like the barn."

Once again Chris was surprised by Lizzie, pleasantly so. "Hi, Mr. Miller. I'm Liz. And you shouldn't have worried about the barn. I'm pretty used to it."

He nodded. "So you're the reason our Chris has run off to Dallas." He winked at Chris. "I can see why, son."

Chris was expecting Lizzie's blush and sure enough, the pink hue blossomed on her cheeks. "We figured it was time you met," Chris began, unsure of where to insert the details into the conversation. Now or after dinner? Or during?

"What do you do, Liz? Chris never really said."

Lizzie's gaze swerved to his and he half shrugged. "It didn't come up," he explained, though he knew he'd kept it a bit quiet. Not for any reason other than they had kept their relationship fairly secret until the last week or two.

"I'm Lizzie Baron," she explained. When no one answered, she added, "I'm the acting president of Baron Energies at the moment."

"Baron Energies?" Bob's jaw dropped. "The oil company?"

She nodded.

"But Brock Baron always ran that. Chris, you competed against his boys, didn't you?"

"Sure did. Jet's good, but Jacob is phenomenal. He could end up with a title this year."

"My dad was injured in an event on the seniors' tour," Lizzie explained. "I'm only heading things up until he can come back to the office. I usually head the Human Resources department."

Which was still a pretty impressive resume in itself, Chris added mentally.

Lizzie took a drink of tea and smiled at his parents, who were still obviously trying to absorb the fact that Lizzie had a rather high-profile position. "Rodeo is how Chris and I met, actually. He was competing the same weekend as my brothers."

He reached over and took her hand. A show of solidarity. Of…affection. Not long ago it had been only a show. Now there was more. A lot more. He'd found that moving in with her had been nearly seamless. Ever since they'd agreed to try seeing each other, taking things slowly without making demands on the future, they'd gotten on extremely well.

The only problem was, Chris *wanted* to make demands. He wanted to make plans. Damn it, he wanted to be with her, and he was scared to tell her in case she pushed him away entirely. He felt as if he was standing on a knife edge. One wrong move and he'd wreck everything.

"I have to admit, we were plenty surprised when Chris said he was taking a year off to compete again. We were also pleased when he went back to his job, even if the promotion took him further away." This from his father, who, Chris realized, was looking pleased as punch that his son had given up the crazy idea of rodeo.

Lizzie squeezed his hand, though, and leaned into his shoulder a little bit. "Well, as long as he's happy. I don't think it really matters what a person does, as long as they enjoy it."

He was surprised at the support she was giving him right now. Even more surprised at the challenge she'd politely issued to his father, all while smiling sweetly.

Bob leaned forward. "Pardon my bluntness, but that's probably easier to say when you've been brought up a Baron."

Chris tensed. This wasn't how things were supposed to go! They still had to break the news about the baby. He tightened his fingers on Lizzie's, a silent warning.

But Lizzie relaxed against his arm and once more turned her warm smile on his dad. "Yes, that's true. But I wouldn't be part of the business if I didn't want to be. I love what I do. I love the company. My brother, on the other hand, isn't so interested in the energy sector and has his own ranch close to Roughneck. My sister runs the farm store." She leaned forward a little. "The one thing we were taught growing up? The value of hard work. There's never been a job any of us was too good for, you know? We all did our fair share of washing dishes and cleaning stalls. Our silver spoon was shaped like a shovel."

Bob's eyes lit with a new respect. "I'm glad to hear it."

She laughed a little and Chris let her take the lead. She was winning over his dad in exactly the right way.

"The one thing I've learned about your son in the time we've been...together?" Chris caught the slight hesitation and hoped his parents hadn't. Lizzie continued on, "He is hardworking, honorable and is determined to live up to his responsibilities. You raised a good man."

Chris watched as his dad sat back a bit, satisfied, and his mom beamed from her chair across the narrow verandah. More than that, though, he felt a warm glow within himself at her words. Was that really how she saw him? As a good man? Honorable? He tried. God knows he tried. And if he'd had to sacrifice some of his happiness, it was worth it.

"You're the first girl Chris has brought home since Erica," his mother said, her eyes shining. "Now we can see why."

There it was. The stamp of approval, even if his mom had brought Erica into the conversation. One thing was for certain, he didn't have to worry about Lizzie wanting him for what he could provide for her. She could manage stability all on her own.

So why was she here? Really? It wasn't about amicable coparenting anymore, hadn't been for a while. Was she starting to truly care for him the way he cared for her?

"There's another reason why," he said softly, looking over at Lizzie for permission to give them the news. She smiled softly and nodded and his heart pounded. Had he just thought the word *care* with regards to Lizzie? It was more than that. He was falling in love with her. Head over heels, stupid in love with her.

He faced his parents, and his chest felt as if it was expanding with…what? Pride? Happiness? He couldn't be sure, but he smiled and said the words.

"We're having a baby."

Shock registered on his parents' faces, and his mother was the first to speak. "A baby?"

"Yes," Lizzie answered. "Around the middle of October."

"Oh, my stars."

"You're going to be a grandma," Chris said, grinning. "Better get your knitting needles out."

"A baby," she repeated. "Oh, honey. It's so fast, but you look happy…." She looked at Lizzie. "I know your family probably doesn't expect it, but we'd like to help with the wedding."

Lizzie froze next to him and he took a breath. "That's a little premature." He tried to keep the mood light and upbeat. "We're just taking things one day at a time for now."

"One day at a time. What does that mean?" This from his dad, who'd sat quietly for the past thirty seconds.

Chris started to speak but Lizzie put a hand on his arm to forestall him and spoke instead. "I know it's not ideal, but I just stopped being sick every morning, and pretty soon I'll be showing. We're still getting used to the idea ourselves, and my dad is mostly in a wheelchair at this point. Not to mention I'm running the company in his absence. We just decided to deal with everything going on first. There's plenty without adding on the stress of a wedding, too."

"You're having a baby, you should be married," Bob insisted.

"Bob," Debra chastised quietly.

"Well, they should."

"This wasn't really planned, Dad," Chris said. "And I would want Lizzie to have a beautiful wedding day and not a rushed justice of the peace deal at the courthouse, you know?"

He could feel Lizzie's gaze on him and wondered if he was so transparent she could see what he was feeling right now. That the idea of marriage no longer scared him as it had once. He figured if she could really see that, she'd be hightailing it in the other direction.

His dad still didn't seem happy and his mom's eyes were worried. "Hey," he said gently, "I know it isn't the way you would have wanted. But that doesn't mean it's not a blessing, okay?"

"I was taken by surprise," Lizzie added. "And afraid. But Chris has been there for me from the first moment. He's right. It *is* a blessing."

He looked over at her and she at him. And in that moment he knew. He was in it all the way. Heart, body and soul. And then she smiled at him and he put his arm around her shoulders, pulling her close.

When he released her, his father's face had softened and his mom had tears in her eyes.

"Well, then, congratulations." Debra got up and came over to the swing, bending down to give Chris a hug. She let him go and turned to Lizzie. "To you, too, dear." And she hugged Lizzie, as well.

After his mom let Lizzie go, she cleared her throat. "I'd better get supper on the go. We have celebrating to do."

Lizzie got up from the swing. "Let me help you. My fried chicken never turns out. Maybe you've got a secret to share."

When the porch door clapped shut behind them, Bob

finally said what was on his mind. "I expect you to do the right thing, Christopher."

"It's not that simple," Chris answered.

"It damn well is." Bob's brows knit together. "You have an obligation...."

Chris's temper snapped and he forced himself to keep his voice calm. "I know very well what my obligations are," he answered tightly. "And I'll do this on my own time and in my own way. Without interference."

His dad raised one eyebrow. "Do you love her, son?"

Chris's throat tightened. "More than I realized," he replied quietly, looking over at the porch door. "And if you taught me anything, it was to do things the right way and not the fastest way. Trust me on this."

Chapter Thirteen

The condo was dark when they got back from Chris's parents'. Lizzie opened the door and flicked a switch, turning on a soft lamp in the living room. A plastic container held leftover fried chicken, given to them by Debra who'd insisted her secret ingredient was seasoning salt. Chris was behind her and he shut the door and locked it for the night.

He was a part of her life now. They'd made the pact to take it slow. To not make promises or plans. But now she was wishing he would.

"Your parents are nice. They love you very much, I could tell."

He chuckled behind her. "And you handled my father perfectly. He respects someone who'll look him in the eye."

She put the chicken in the fridge and turned around. "So do I. I know he pushed you to be something you didn't want…."

"If I'd hated it, I would have done something else. Really, Lizzie, it's not that big a deal. I understand where he's coming from."

"I meant what I said, too. You should do what makes you happy. If it's rodeo, it's rodeo. If it's working with horses, you should do that. I know you feel you have obligations, but that doesn't have to come down to a dollar sign, you know?"

"Maybe it's pride," he suggested, and she noticed he was frowning a little.

"Why, because I make more than you? I don't care about that. God, Chris. Don't be such a snob." She knew it sounded strange, considering she was the one who ran in different circles than he did, but pride could be a foolish thing to hang on to now and again.

"You don't think people will say I latched on to you for your money?"

She frowned now as he zeroed in on what had been one of her greatest fears. "Who cares what people say?"

"Maybe I do. I know what it's like to be with someone who wants you for what you can provide, and not for who you are. Granted, I didn't have Baron prestige behind me but I had a good job and a good income and stability and Erica saw that as her ticket. And when I announced I was taking a year off, she wasn't quite so interested."

"I don't see you that way."

"Oh? So the fact that I'm practically living in *your* condo doesn't look the least bit opportunistic?"

"No!" She was truly confused now. The one thing she'd liked about him from the start was that he hadn't seemed to care that her last name was Baron. "Where the hell is all this coming from?" They still stood in the space between the kitchen and living room, faced off, not quite an argument but not a relaxed conversation either.

"I'm sorry." He let out a huge breath. "I get crazy when I'm with my dad. He's got very strong opinions about a man's responsibilities."

She went to him then, took his hands in hers. She probably shouldn't have left him alone with his dad this afternoon. Chris had been quiet during dinner—not incredibly so, but enough that she'd noticed he was a bit subdued. What in the world had his father said to him that had dampened his mood so much?

"You know that I turned down Mark Baker when I was in college," she began quietly. "That was my strong moment. I could see he was only really interested in me as a Baron. And while he's not my favorite person, I know he's very good at his job and we've moved past that awkward beginning. But what you don't know is that I turned him down because I'd learned a hard lesson the year before."

"I don't understand."

"You're sensitive because of your past experience, and so am I. I got my heart broken in college, Chris. My family isn't stupid rich but we're well enough off. I let myself get caught up in a relationship with a law student, fell in love. At the end of my third year he proposed and I was in heaven. And that was when it started. He started talking about the wedding guest list and the people he wanted to invite for their connections. I started fourth year and was trying to study and he was all about appearances together and being seen. Everything had to be just so. And then he started referring to us as the Texas power couple and I knew he was only half joking. He kept saying that with his ambition and Lizzie Baron on his arm, he'd be in congress by the time he was thirty-five."

"Liz," Chris said quietly. "That's horrible."

"I flat-out asked him if he really loved me. And he said he did, but it wasn't in his eyes. I got his politician smile and charming assurances and I knew it wasn't real. He broke my heart."

"What did you do?"

"Broke off the engagement, much to my family's relief. Focused on my studies and when word circulated that *he'd* been the one to break it off, I let it go. He wanted to come out of it smelling like a rose. I'd dodged a bullet. It didn't really matter who'd done the kicking to the curb."

"I'm sorry," he offered weakly. "And then Mark came along?"

She smiled then. "Yeah. And I could see him coming a mile away. Fool me once… Anyway, my point is, if you were latching on to me for my name, I'd know it. And I don't see that at all. I see someone who got caught up in something unexpected, who's making the best of it, and being pretty wonderful when all is said and done. So no, it doesn't bother me that our paychecks might not match. I couldn't care less."

She wasn't sure what she expected after her little speech, but it wasn't the glow in his eyes as he moved closer and put his hand on her face, caressing her cheekbone with his thumb.

"Do you know how extraordinary you are?" he murmured. "I think I'm the one who landed in clover here."

"You say that until I'm big as a barn with swollen ankles and a disposition like a raging bull."

"Am I still going to be here then, Liz?"

"Do you want to be?"

She held her breath, waiting for his answer. They'd said no plans. But he'd asked. And she'd asked the more important question. Because she didn't want him to leave. She liked seeing him first thing in the morning. She was happy to be home with him at night, looking at real estate, having someone across the table from her as she ate dinner, to curl up to at night. It wasn't just the sex, even though that was where they'd started. It was more. So much more.

"Yes," he breathed. "I think I do want to be here. Very much."

Her pulse leapt. "We're doing this then? Us?"

His smile, the one she loved, slightly lopsided that popped his dimple, appeared. "Yeah, we're doing this."

He kissed her, but this time it was different. It was filled with the potential for both happiness and failure. It was fragile, too, holding both their hearts in the balance as they stepped off into something unknown. And for Lizzie, it was truly the beginning of something she hadn't felt in a very long time—love. And that love came from trust. Trust that her heart was safe with him.

She took his hand and led him to the bedroom. Silently, with their gazes locked, they undressed. Lizzie sensed they were at a turning point where everything from this moment would be different. They weren't falling into anything like they had before, or easing into it like they had his moving in. They had made a conscious decision to be together—really together. To meet as equals, face-to-face, heart-to-heart. It was so much bigger than it had ever been before, scary in its awesomeness.

Chris came forward and reached for her, his fingers grazing over the slight bump of her stomach. Their baby. Theirs. Right now it was feeling like a miracle—a perfect little person growing inside her, half Lizzie and half Chris.

And when they made love the emotion overwhelmed her heart. She was in love with him, she realized, a tear forming at the corner of her eye. With this strong, noble, gentle man who had accidentally fathered her child.

Minutes later, curled up in his embrace under the covers, she closed her eyes and felt a prayer of thanks. She'd never imagined she'd find someone like him, especially when she wasn't even looking. It was all going to work out just fine, she thought, slipping into the relaxed state just before sleep. It would all be fine with Chris at her side.

LEAVING FOR WORK the next morning was different than other mornings. Instead of a brief "have a nice day," she kissed Chris goodbye at his truck and then walked the few blocks to the DART station to catch her train. She'd only made it halfway to the office when she got a text from him saying simply see you tonight, xx. She smiled to herself as she answered back and asked what he wanted to do for dinner.

But once she was at the office she squared her shoulders and got her head in the game. She had a full day planned, including talking to Jacob about safety inspection practices. Despite Brock's defiance, she fully planned to help Jacob move into a bigger role within the company. Once Brock realized how valuable he was, he'd come around. She was sure of it. Right now it felt as if anything was possible.

She was halfway to her office when Maria fell into step with her. "I need to see you right away," the older woman said, her expression serious. "Something came by courier this morning that you're going to want to look at."

That didn't sound good. Lizzie frowned. "What?"

"This." Maria handed over an envelope and Lizzie slid the sheaf of papers out, scanning the top page.

It took her a moment to realize what she was holding and when she did her feet stopped moving and her blood ran cold. "You've got to be kidding me."

"Nicole Bennett from AB Windpower has already phoned and set up a meeting with you for this afternoon."

"This afternoon?" Lizzie checked her watch. So little time. And then there was the fact that the company involved was the same company Chris worked for. Coincidence? Not likely. But thinking about the possibilities made her body feel numb and she couldn't afford that right now. She had to deal with one emergency at a time. And she had to prepare. That was the most important thing.

"Do you want me to reschedule?" Maria asked, her eyes worried.

"No, I don't think so," Lizzie replied, starting down the hall again with Maria keeping pace beside her. She needed to find out more before she went home tonight. Hearing what this Ms. Bennett woman had to say would be a good place to start. "Can you reschedule my day though so I can get through this and do a little research? I don't want to be on the back foot going into this meeting."

They stopped in front of Lizzie's office and Maria fidgeted, standing by the door instead of going on her way. "What is it, Maria? You look like you want to say something."

"Maybe you should call your dad. Or have someone from the board sit in with you."

"And have Ms. Bennett think that I'm not capable of taking a meeting on my own?" Lizzie raised an eyebrow. She really wanted to approach this from a position of power, and how could she do that if she brought in a team of reinforcements as though she was afraid? "I want to take this first meeting solo. And then I'll bring everyone in, I promise. All this will be is taking the temperature of the situation." She frowned. "Can you find out a little bit about Nicole Bennett for me?"

"I'll see what I can dig up. But Lizzie…" Maria put her hand on Lizzie's arm. "I've known your father for a long time. Don't keep him in the dark, or it'll blow up in your face. Let him help you."

"I will. I just want to go to him with a full picture," she promised, but there was a dark feeling in the pit of her stomach. She should have mentioned something to Brock about the stock activity when Mark first came to her. Good heavens, was AB Windpower behind that, too? Were they coming at Baron from all sides? And what did Chris know about this?

Once she was in her office she shut her door and went to her desk, reading the document as she sat down. She understood how merging the smaller company with the larger one might strengthen AB's financial position, but it was odd that a company established to market alternative energy solutions wanted to be joined with oil and gas. It was counterintuitive, wasn't it? It just seemed that in the current trend, AB was taking a step backward by seeking an alliance with Baron.

She tapped her fingers on her desk. Then again, Lizzie had expressed an opinion about diversifying, hadn't she? She loved Baron Energies but thought there was a huge opportunity to take a "whole energy solution" approach to the future rather than picking sides.

She'd expressed an opinion and on more than one occasion, though not since taking over the presidency. Suddenly her body went cold as she thought back to the conversations she'd had in private with Chris. Had she said as much to him? Because having him so close to her and having this proposal cross her desk only weeks later seemed a little too convenient to be coincidental.

She didn't want to believe it. Not of him. But suddenly little things started adding up.

He had been on his leave until she told him who she was, and then he'd immediately gone back to work. And he'd garnered himself a promotion in the process. More than once she'd mentioned wanting to move into alternative energy. She'd even mentioned the stock issue and her worries about it.

The truth slapped her across the face. Oh, my God, had she done it again? Gotten herself tangled up with a man who was far more interested in her name than in her? And now she would be tied to him forever, wouldn't she? Because there would always be their child between them.

Her stomach turned sickeningly.

She would get to the bottom of it later, and deal with one crisis at a time. The first one was preparing for her meeting with Nicole Bennett. For that she had to be at the top of her game.

NICOLE BENNETT WAS one of the most beautiful women Lizzie had ever seen. She was close to Lizzie's age, give or take a year or two and petite, with a glorious mane of dark brown hair that was twisted up into a tidy chignon at the base of her neck. A few artfully arranged tendrils spiraled whimsically by her ears, and her skin was flawless. Her figure was packaged perfectly in an off-white skirt and blazer with trim a shade darker. The two tones were repeated in her heels, and she carried an expensive leather satchel in a perfectly manicured hand.

Lizzie, on the other hand, had popped the button on her skirt during a bathroom break and was in constant fear of the zipper letting go. Her blouse felt a little too tight across her breasts, too, although she'd taken ten minutes to freshen up in the bathroom and had tidied her hair and touched up her makeup.

"Ms. Bennett," Lizzie greeted, holding out her hand

and trying not to feel like the ugly, awkward stepsister. "Please come in."

Lizzie showed Nicole into a small boardroom. It was no less luxurious than the big room, but on a smaller scale. Rich wood furniture, comfortable chairs, photo prints of the ranch on the walls. A carafe of coffee and a pitcher of water were set in the middle of the table, along with a plate of pastries.

Ms. Bennett had to know she was on Baron turf here.

Once they were seated Lizzie folded her hands on the table. "What can I do for you today, Ms. Bennett?"

Nicole smiled and took her time answering, instead reaching for the water pitcher. "Do you mind if I have a drink? It's hot out there today."

"Oh, of course. Help yourself."

Lizzie forced herself to wait patiently as Nicole poured a glass of iced water and took a few sips. "Better," Nicole smiled, relaxing a little. "It's good to finally meet you, Ms. Baron."

Which meant that Nicole knew who Lizzie was, while Lizzie was pretty much in the dark about Nicole—other than the basic details from her AB Windpower bio, which stated her role at the company as well as her academic background.

"Likewise," she replied, reaching for the second glass and pouring some water. She was suddenly feeling very dry. There were questions she wanted to ask and it was hell trying to bide her time.

"You're probably wondering about the proposal we sent over." Nicole smiled at her, then reached into her satchel and took out a file. When she opened it, Lizzie recognized the top sheet as the same document she'd received by courier only hours before.

"You're the one who requested the meeting," Lizzie reminded her coolly. "Danish?"

"No, thank you." Nicole leaned forward a little. "Lizzie, I'm not here to confront or threaten you. You can relax."

Lizzie merely raised an eyebrow. "Then why are you here? I've been through your proposal. It's interesting reading for sure, but I can't understand why you'd want to merge with an oil company. It practically goes against your mission statement."

Something flickered across Nicole's face, but she cleared it quickly. "Baron's profile is strong. It would be financially beneficial for us to merge with your company. There would be significant benefits to us, as Baron is a publicly traded company."

"But why us, and why now?"

Lizzie had read the report. She knew what was in it. But it was different seeing someone face-to-face. She'd worked in HR long enough to know the value of in-person meetings. There were nuances that simply couldn't be gleaned from a black-and-white document. And right now Ms. Bennett appeared confident but a bit rehearsed.

"You've said yourself that you're interested in alternative forms of energy. Besides, Baron lost that contract in the Gulf not long ago. We're in a unique position to help each other."

Except Baron's position wasn't *that* weakened.

"One contract is hardly a significant event," Lizzie reminded her. Well, maybe it was somewhat significant, but it certainly hadn't put the company in a precarious position.

"One contract on top of a president and CEO who is recuperating away from the office and the picture for Baron Energies isn't quite as rosy as it was even a few months ago." Nicole took a sip of water. "Your stock position has weakened significantly."

Lizzie's ears pricked up at that, but she forced herself to remain calm and detached. "The stock is rebounding."

"There's been a lot of trade activity."

Lizzie frowned, her composure slipping. "And would AB know anything about that?"

"What?" Nicole's face changed, too. "What do you mean?"

"What I'm asking is, has AB Windpower been buying up Baron stock? Are you planning a reverse takeover if the merger doesn't go through?"

Nicole's face blanked. Lizzie had taken her by surprise, then. Good. She'd either try to cover her tracks or be at a loss, knowing nothing about it. Lizzie watched her carefully. She might not be CEO material, but she knew how to read people....

Except Christopher, a small voice inside her head reminded her. If her suspicions were correct, she'd misread him utterly...

"I don't know anything about stock purchases or any sort of takeover attempt. Everything that AB Windpower proposes is right there in the document I sent you. If we'd been buying up stock, I'd know about it. Trust me."

Lizzie asked one more question, hoping to throw Nicole off guard. "Nicole, why are you here instead of your boss? Who is Adele Black and why did she send you?"

And there it was. She covered it well, but for the breath of a second there was fear in Nicole Bennett's eyes. Lizzie's curiosity was piqued now. There was definitely more to this company than what she saw on the surface. And there was Christopher, right in the middle of it. Damn it.

"Ms. Black is the head of our company, but unfortunately she's been ill the past few days." Nicole's eyes shifted away to her papers and she tidied them up before looking at Lizzie again. "I'm here in her place. My words stand as her words."

"Interesting that my father's illness was just mentioned as weakening our company's position," Lizzie pointed out, feeling in control once more. "Of course I'll be taking this proposal to the board of directors, but I wouldn't get my hopes up too high."

"Thanks for fitting me into your schedule." Nicole closed her file and tucked it in her satchel. She held out her hand and smiled. "It was good to finally meet you, Lizzie."

Lizzie shook Nicole's hand and smiled back. She wanted to keep it impersonal but the truth was she rather liked Ms. Bennett's style. They were also the same age, both women in the same male-dominated industry and Lizzie suspected they had a lot in common.

She dropped her hand. "It was good to meet you, too, Nicole. I'm sure we'll meet again."

"You can count on it." Nicole handed over a card. "I'll be in town for a couple of days. You can contact me at that cell number if you want to talk further."

Lizzie knew she wouldn't. "Can I show you the way out?"

Nicole shook her head. "No, I can find my way just fine. I'm sure you have a busy schedule."

She left the boardroom and Lizzie followed a moment later after gathering up her file. She wanted to return to her own office to gather her thoughts before calling her dad—she'd need to see him and soon to keep him up-to-date with what was going on. She was just passing the reception desk when she spied Nicole by the elevators, talking on her cell phone.

"Yes, I met her," Nicole said, holding the phone against her ear as she searched for something in her purse. "And she's just as lovely as you said she would be. Determined, too."

Lizzie's cheeks flooded with heat. God, who was she talking to? Chris? He was the only one she could think of who would have a connection between the two of them.

She went directly to her office. "Emory, I don't want to be disturbed for a while, okay?" She said the words as she passed by her assistant's desk.

"Are you okay, Lizzie?" Emory's head popped up from where she'd been staring at her monitor.

"I just need a few minutes."

Emory popped up and followed Lizzie to her door. "Is it the baby?" she asked quietly. "Can I get you something? Do you need to lie down?"

Lizzie was perilously close to crying now that the meeting was over and the truth was too close to ignore. "How did you know?" she asked, her voice catching.

Emory's eyes were sympathetic. "The morning trips to the bathroom were a major clue, along with no more morning coffee runs. And I've seen you touching your tummy sometimes when you don't think anyone is watching." She smiled gently. "I used to do that all the time when I was expecting Jeremiah."

Lizzie nodded, her emotions suddenly getting the best of her. "I'm okay. I just need to regroup."

"I'm going to bring you some tea," Emory stated. "And something to eat. I'll hold all your calls until you say otherwise."

"Thanks, Em."

"No problem. And congratulations." Emory gave a small smile and backed out of Lizzie's office, closing the door behind her.

Lizzie turned away from her desk and went to the small sofa that sat along one wall. She often used it to read over reports and evaluations, but today she simply tucked in her feet and hugged a throw pillow, closing her eyes.

When she had herself together, she'd have to call her dad. And she'd have to admit how much she'd screwed up.

And then she'd go home and deal with Chris.

Chapter Fourteen

Chris let himself into the condo, using his key with his right hand and holding his laptop bag and a bag of groceries in the other. He'd stopped at a deli and picked up the Thai salad that Lizzie had liked so much the last time they were there. They'd have a quick dinner and then chill for a while. Maybe take a walk around University Park and get some fresh air. Hold hands.

The house was quiet when he walked in. He frowned. Lizzie must be working late. He wished she wouldn't since she seemed to tire easier these days, but he understood the pressure she was under. He dropped his bag by the sofa and went into the kitchen to put the food in the fridge.

He had his head half in the refrigerator when she spoke behind him. "You're home," she said quietly, scaring him to death. He jumped and shut the door to the fridge.

"Gosh, you're quiet. You must have stealthy cat feet." He grinned at her, but his grin faded when he realized she wasn't smiling back. Were her eyes a little bit red? Unease rippled through him as he looked closer. "Lizzie, what's wrong? Is it the baby?"

He saw her swallow. Then he saw past her to what sat on the floor in the living room.

His duffel bag.

What the…?

"That's my bag," he said numbly.

"Yes, it is. I'd like you to leave."

His eyes opened wider. "You what? Liz, what's going on?"

"Don't call me that!" she snapped.

She had been crying. Something was desperately wrong. Just this morning he'd texted her something sweet and she'd replied asking about dinner plans. Now she was staring at him like he was a cockroach crossing the dinner table. With disgust. Revulsion.

"What has happened?" He took a step forward but she stepped back and he put up his hands. "Okay. You're upset. I get it. Just tell me what's going on. I'm really starting to worry here."

Her dark eyes accused him. "How well do you know Nicole Bennett?"

Nicole? What did she have to do with all of this?

"Quite well. She's the VP of Operations at AB Windpower."

"You're not denying it, then."

"Denying what?" The thought running through his mind was so ludicrous he couldn't help but laugh a little. "You think there's something between me and Nicole?"

"She's certainly pretty enough. All that gorgeous hair and her tiny waist and…and…"

"Lizzie," he said gently. "I'm with you."

He reached for her again but she recoiled. "No, no you're not." She pinned him with her angry stare again. "Did Nicole give you your promotion?"

"Yes, we met for coffee and she offered it to me. But they'd offered it before I took my leave, too, and I turned it down…."

"How convenient that the moment you decided you wanted to go back to work you not only got your job back but a transfer and a management position. What'd you have to do to score that, Miller?"

God above, she was angry and he couldn't figure out why. "You're not making any sense. Are you asking if Nicole and I had an affair? How do you even know what she looks like?"

"I got a good look when she was in my boardroom earlier today."

His blood chilled even though he still couldn't figure out exactly what had happened here. "Why was Nicole in your boardroom?" he asked slowly.

"Like you don't know. Save the innocent act, Chris. I don't have time for it."

She turned away and went to the window in the living room, looking out over the city and toward the downtown.

Nicole had gone to Baron Energies and had a meeting with Lizzie. Chris had no idea why. But what was crystal clear was that Lizzie thought he did. She thought he was part of it.

"What did she want?" he asked, following her. "What is it you think I did?"

She swiveled around. "You know, I thought you were different. You *were* different—for one night only. But the moment you found out who I was…you're just like all the rest." Her eyes glistened with angry tears. "I should have listened to my instincts in the first place. Just take your stuff and get out. We'll talk about custody and visitation when the time comes."

She'd totally gone off the rails. "What the hell did Nicole tell you today?"

"You're really going to make me say it? Fine." She

strode across the room to her briefcase and took out a sheaf of papers. "Tell me how it's a complete coincidence that the company you work for, the company who recently gave you a fat promotion, just happens to be proposing a merger with Baron Energies!"

"A merger? Between AB and Baron? Are you sure?"

"Oh, for Pete's sake. Would I be this upset if I wasn't sure?" She waggled the papers in front of him. "Read for yourself if you don't believe me."

He took the papers. Scanned the first few pages, but it was a bunch of legalese he would need to sit down to decipher. "I believe you," he said, handing it back. And he did. She was right. She wouldn't be this upset if she weren't sure. "But, Lizzie, I don't know anything about it."

She snorted. "Sure. Know what I learned a long time ago? There's no such thing as a coincidence. I just happen to get together with you. I mention..." She broke off, shook her head. Her voice was thick as she continued, "I mention how I'd like to diversify our holdings and how I keep hitting a brick wall with Dad. And then weeks later, after your nice, plush assignment, I get slammed with this using practically those exact words! That I have supported the idea of alternative energies before and now that my dad isn't at the helm..."

She gulped in air. "It was a good exchange for you. A little information and a nice payoff. The stock dip after the accident and lost contract was bad enough. But this... I should have known better."

She actually thought he'd fed information to Nicole and Adele. That he'd used her.

"I'm not him," he said firmly, getting a little angry himself.

"Not who?"

Her hands were on her hips now. Despite the red-rimmed eyes, she looked amazing all fired up. Strong and determined, an avenging angel. It was just too bad she was accusing him of something he hadn't done.

"The guy in college. The one you were engaged to who was using you for your family connections. Not everyone has an ulterior motive."

She shook her head. "I should never have come to find you that day. I should have just left well enough alone."

"And not tell me I have a son or daughter? Are you serious?" He paced, trying to sort out his thoughts and say what was racing through his mind without sounding like a raging lunatic, but what she was implying was really sinking in now. He'd been getting bucked off horses and having a marvelous time when she'd come in and turned his world upside down…for what? This?

He stopped and faced her. "I told you I was thinking of leaving the industry altogether."

"Convenient."

He frowned. "Lizzie, listen to yourself. For God's sake. I was going from rodeo to rodeo. I was surprised as anything when I found out who you were."

"Didn't take you long to capitalize on it though."

"Stop. Just stop." He raised his voice a little and took a breath, quieting again. "I didn't do what you're saying I did. Why would I? I turned down that management job once before and I did it for good reasons. The only reason I took it was so that I could be closer to you and the baby. So I could provide both of you with the kind of life a man should provide for his child and his…his…"

"His what?" she asked quietly.

"I thought we were figuring that out," he replied. "But I did think we were *something*."

"A fraud," she said blandly. "We let our families believe we had this great courtship when we didn't. We hooked up and it was an accident. And now I have to live with the consequences forever."

"Lizzie, I swear to you. I didn't breathe a word about you to Nicole." And yet as he said it, he remembered Nicole mentioning the Barons at their coffee date when she'd offered him the job. In the interest of full disclosure, he brought it up. "She asked me once if I knew the family well, but it was because of the boys and rodeo, not because of you. She doesn't even know we're together."

"We're not," Lizzie answered.

Anger flared now. "You know what? This isn't about me. It's about you. It's about being too damn scared to trust anyone to hang around. And you hide behind the Baron name as a means of escape. So what if one person used you? You kicked him to the curb. And now you use that for your excuse any time someone gets too close. Because what you're really afraid of is being betrayed. Being pushed aside. Being…disposable. You're afraid everyone is going to walk away just like your mom did."

Numb silence filled the room for several moments until Lizzie took a deep breath. "You should go."

Yes, he probably should, especially since he heard the quiver in her voice. That last bit had hurt her and he hadn't wanted to, but what did she expect? He'd trusted her, too. He'd started to care about her and the baby so much. He'd been falling in love with her, hadn't he? And now he knew exactly how much she'd trusted and cared for him, didn't he? What a fool he'd been, turning his life upside down in order to do the right thing. Every single time he'd done that in his life, he made himself unhappy.

He went to her then and put his hands on her arms. She trembled beneath his touch and regret flooded through him. "I swear on our baby, I had nothing to do with the proposal from AB Windpower. I never knew it was in the works, never heard a word about it. I asked for the transfer so I could be close to you and the baby, and that's the only reason. It's up to you whether or not you believe me."

He let go and retrieved the duffel she'd so helpfully packed before he'd arrived home. It weighed extra heavy as he carried it to the door. He put his hand on the knob but turned around. "Someday, Lizzie, you're going to have to put your faith in someone. Otherwise you'll always be alone."

There was an odd sort of stinging behind his eyes as he looked at her standing there, pitiful and lost. "I know you, sweetheart. That's not the way you want to live your life."

He opened the door and shut it behind him and then started down the hall. He was taking a chance right now. She wanted him gone—or at least she thought she did, but he walked slowly down the hall to the elevator. Any moment now she'd open the door and come after him, say she was sorry for blaming him, ask him to come back and talk it out. And he'd hold her in his arms and they'd put the pieces back together.

He got to the elevator and there was no sound. No door opening. No nothing.

And still he waited in front of the closed elevator doors, hoping.

Several minutes later he called himself the biggest fool on earth and pushed the down button.

LIZZIE WRESTLED WITH the skirt zipper once more and then gave up and reached for the tailored pants with the flat waistband and the peasant-style blouse that camouflaged her changing figure. Her wardrobe was really becoming a challenge as her shape changed but she was still too small for maternity clothes. Besides, the news was still limited to family and, of course, Emory, who would rather die than reveal Lizzie's secret. She trusted her assistant completely.

She took her bagged lunch from the fridge and put it in her tote bag, then went out the door for the walk in the May sunshine to the train. Got on and thought about the day's itinerary on the ride to the office. Got off the train and walked the short distance to the high-rise that housed Baron Energies.

She was going through the motions and she knew it.

After Chris had departed, she hadn't quite known what to do with herself, so she called Maria and got her to set up a board meeting for the following day. She'd offered to drive out to the ranch to speak to her father first, but Brock had a follow-up appointment with his orthopedic surgeon in the city anyway, and Julieta had relented and agreed to bring him by.

Lizzie knew the moment he'd arrived because she could hear him grumbling about his wheelchair all the way down the hall. Smiling to herself, she stuck her head out of her office and saw the procession approaching—Brock, in the evil chair, Julieta, with the patience of Job pushing him along, and Maria, carrying a tray with coffee for the three of them.

"Small boardroom work for you?" Lizzie called out.

Brock looked up and a smile spread across his face. "There she is. How're you feeling, Mama? That man of yours treating you right?"

She tried to ignore the pain that slashed through her at the well-intended words and pasted on a smile. Brock and Julieta both frowned at her tepid reaction while Lizzie noticed Maria's mouth hanging open with surprise. "I'm feeling fine, Dad. Come on in."

While Julieta got Brock settled, Maria put down the tray and approached Lizzie. "Sweetie, I didn't know. I wish you'd told me."

"I didn't want anyone to know, Maria, but thank you." Nerves began to bubble as she realized she would soon be telling Brock everything. "Do you think you could get me some orange juice though? I've been craving it all morning." In a way it was a relief to have a few people know and not have to watch every word or action.

"Sure I can." She slipped out and shut the door behind her.

Julieta gave Brock a kiss on the cheek. "I'll be in my office if you need me. Be good."

He patted her hand, then gave it a squeeze. "Lizzie'll take care of me."

When Julieta was gone, Lizzie took the seat across from her father.

"What's going on, Lizzie? Most of the time you try to avoid my input."

"Sorry, Dad," she apologized, a little embarrassed.

"Don't be. I'm going crazy feeling useless and you're trying to be independent. I'm not stupid."

She sighed. "Some stuff has been going on and I should have talked to you about it before."

His brows pulled together. "Why didn't you?"

Guilt spiraled through her. "Because I wanted to deal with it on my own. Because I didn't want to think about stuff happening to Baron while I was at the wheel."

"Lizzie, what in God's name haven't you told me?"

Maria knocked and came back in with a bottle of orange juice and a glass for Lizzie. While Lizzie poured it, Brock helped himself to a cup of coffee. Maria left quietly, Lizzie took a fortifying drink and faced her father.

"A few weeks ago Mark Baker came to me with some

information. It wasn't anything too serious, just something to keep our eye on."

"I know you don't trust Mark."

"I don't like Mark. There's a difference. I do, however, think he's very good at his job. We dealt well enough together."

Brock gave a short nod.

"It was expected that our stock would take a dip, both after the lost contract and then when you had your accident, so seeing those numbers wasn't a surprise. What was a surprise was the level of activity following that dip. Not alarming, but it was something that flagged for Mark and he came to me about it. We agreed it was something we'd keep an eye on."

Brock's face looked concerned. "And? I take it that's not all."

"And that takes us to part two, which was a meeting I had yesterday."

"I don't think I like the sound of this."

"I received a document by courier first thing yesterday morning, and the sender had already called to set up a meeting to follow up. It was someone from AB Windpower with a merger proposal."

Brock's coffee cup came down on the table, a little of the liquid sloshing over the side. "A merger? Over my dead body."

Lizzie smiled weakly. "I knew you'd say that. And I pretty much did, as well. It seemed strange to me on a lot of levels, actually. I mean, we've taken a hit lately but our position isn't that vulnerable. And it's odd for an alternative energy company to look to join with oil, don't you think? Nicole Bennett—that's who I met with—said part of the reason is to strengthen their market position. We're a publicly traded company, they're not."

"But they could approach any number of companies if that was their main motivation."

"I agree." She took a deep breath. "Dad, I think I might have prompted this without even realizing it."

"What do you mean?" He grabbed a paper napkin from the coffee tray and mopped up the spilled brew.

"I've mentioned before that I wouldn't mind exploring alternative energy solutions, perhaps as a subsidiary. I swear to you, I haven't breathed a word of that since taking over, because I wanted to keep Baron as strong as possible during the transition. At least, I haven't said anything...publicly."

Brock's eyes were keen on her. "What do you mean, publicly?"

She swallowed against the lump in her throat. "I might have mentioned it a few times...in private."

Brock was uncharacteristically quiet, which was much worse than the expected tirade.

"Dad...I said a few things to Christopher in private. I never thought anything of it until yesterday when Nicole was here. Chris works for AB Windpower, Dad, and just got a nice transfer and management position. It's all a little too neat and tidy."

She slumped back in her chair. She felt so stupid and... gullible. And now she felt like a disappointment in her dad's eyes.

"Did you ask Chris about it?" Brock asked, more calmly than she expected.

"He denied it. But then he would, wouldn't he?"

Brock sighed.

"Lizzie, darlin', I'm not saying he did or didn't do it. But this is the man you're having a child with. The man who, by all reports, has basically moved into your home. Now, I don't know all that's gone on between the two of you, and I don't want to. But if there's that much feeling between you, maybe you owe him the benefit of the doubt."

Nothing her father could have said would have surprised her more. "But if he did do it, he's betrayed me. And you. And hurt the company…"

"Honey, he hasn't hurt the company. It was a merger proposal, nothing more. We're not that vulnerable."

"But the stock… I asked Nicole if they were planning on using the back door and attempting a reverse takeover…."

He chuckled. "And she said she didn't know anything about that. Lizzie, Mark came to me after he spoke to you. We looked at the volume and decided it's not enough to really be concerned about. Not enough to attempt a takeover or even voting shares. Plus our stock price has started to bounce back. We both think people are taking advantage of the low price knowing it's going to climb and show great returns. You've been doing a great job here."

She wasn't sure what to feel at this moment. Anger and frustration at Mark, who'd promised to let her talk to Brock on her own time but had gone ahead anyway, not trusting her. Relief that things were okay, and a surprising amount of pride at her father's validating words.

"You never asked me about the stock." She met his gaze. "Why?"

"Because you were handling it. Because I kept trying to run things from home instead of trusting you. Julieta made me see that by doing that, I was undermining your confidence and abilities. I decided to let you take the lead on this one."

"Or you gave me enough rope to hang myself," she added ruefully.

He laughed. "If I'd needed to step in, I would have."

"Dad…" Unexpected tears gathered behind her eyes and clogged her throat. "I… Thank you for that."

"Baron's been in capable hands. It hasn't always been easy to accept. A man likes to think that things might fall apart in his absence. It's not a good feeling to not be needed."

She reached across the table and took his hand. "You'll always be needed. You know that."

He squeezed her hand back. "I hope so. So, what's your next move?"

"I called a board meeting for this afternoon. Do you want to stick around for that, or are you heading home?"

He slid his hand away from hers. "It's all yours. I have physio at one-thirty and if I ever want to get permanently out of this chair I have to do what they say. Besides, you know what you're doing."

The unequivocal support was surprising and it buoyed her up more than he could possibly know. "I'll call you tonight with an update."

"That sounds good. Now, about Christopher…"

"Dad…" She wasn't sure she really wanted to take advice about her love life from her dad.

"Maybe you should talk to this Nicole about it. Did you get the impression that she's a straight shooter?"

She thought back. She'd liked the other woman even if they'd been on opposite sides of the table. "Yeah, I did."

Brock hesitated a moment, then leaned forward a little. "I know I'm your dad and I don't usually get into this sort of stuff, but…do you love him, Lizzie?"

She felt like crying. "I did."

But Brock shook his head. "No. If you really loved him, you couldn't turn it off like that. It takes time to get over someone you love. And you mask the pain with anger and hate until it's bearable."

"Like you did with Mom?"

He gave a start at the mention of Delia. "Yes, like your mom," he admitted, looking away for a moment. "What I'm saying is, if you love him, be sure you're ending it for the right reasons and not because you're afraid."

"What would I be afraid of?" she scoffed.

"Of being left again," he said gently. "Of not being the one in control. I've seen you growing up, Lizzie, whether you think I noticed or not. I see how you keep people at arm's length, how you always try to do the right thing and take on the responsibility of the family. But when I saw you with Chris at the ranch that night, I saw a different Lizzie. There was a light in you that had been missing. Be very, very sure before you throw all that away, okay?"

A tear rolled down her cheek. "Okay, Daddy."

She got up and went around the table, bent down to give him a hug. "Thank you for trusting me with this."

"I just want you to be happy, Lizzie. That's all I've ever wanted for all my kids, even though I know they don't always believe it."

"I think we know that, deep down."

He patted her back. "I told Julieta I wouldn't aggravate you for long. And I expect you want to prepare for the meeting."

"Yeah, I do. I'll take you down to her office if you like."

"Sounds good. I hate trying to navigate this damn thing."

She laughed and put her hands on the grips of the wheelchair. "After this, I'm guessing it'll be a while before you try riding bulls, huh?"

"I'm afraid my rodeo days are over," he lamented. "Time to hang up my spurs."

It bothered her that he sounded so down about it. It made her think of Chris and his year of freedom, his one last chance to enjoy the one thing he loved doing. He'd given it all up so quickly, too—for the job in Dallas.

Why? She frowned as she pushed Brock around the corner toward Julieta's office. If it were just about the money, why would he have taken the year off? And he'd already turned down the position once...

Which he'd reminded her of last night, only she'd been too hurt and angry to really hear him.

Was it possible he'd been telling the truth and she'd been too afraid to listen?

"Here we are!" She announced their arrival a little too perkily and Julieta looked up, her lips pursing a little.

"Everything okay?"

"Lizzie's got it handled," Brock announced. "Come on, wife, let me take you to lunch before I go for my torture session."

Lizzie saw the light blush to Julieta's cheeks. Even though they seemed an unlikely pair, Lizzie could see the genuine affection between her father and Julieta. They cared for each other. They were there for each other. And wasn't that what mattered?

"Thanks, Dad," she said, kissing his head. "Especially for the advice."

"Hey, at least one of my children listens to my advice. Maybe there's still hope for the others," he joked.

She left them there deciding on a restaurant for lunch.

Back in her office, she picked up the phone and called the number on Nicole Bennett's card.

Chapter Fifteen

For the second time in as many days, Lizzie found herself face-to-face with Nicole Bennett. They met at a coffee and pie shop simply called Patsy's Pies, away from the office area, closer to Lizzie's home and the University Park area. After ordering, they settled themselves at a corner table.

"Oh, my God," Nicole raved, closing her eyes. "This was the best suggestion. This pie is to die for."

Lizzie looked across the table. Both women still wore their office attire, but chocolate cream pie appeared to be the great equalizer. She couldn't help but grin. "Coconut cream is my other favorite," she admitted. "But really, there's not a pie here that's not ten times better than anywhere else. The hand-pie business is pretty brisk, too." Indeed, several customers took bakery boxes of the individual pies to go.

Nicole took a sip of her latte. "Why did you ask me here, Lizzie? Has there been a change in your position?"

"No, there hasn't. I've met with my father personally and took it to the board, as well. That wasn't why I asked to meet you."

"I see." Nicole put down her cup. "No, actually, I don't see. Why else would you want to talk to me?"

Lizzie took a breath. "It's about Christopher Miller."

"Chris? Why would you want to talk to me about Chris?"

The headache that had been threatening to blossom all day long began to throb behind Lizzie's eyes. "You don't have to pretend you don't know, Nicole."

"Know what?" She genuinely looked perplexed.

"Are you saying that you don't know we're... involved?"

Nicole put down her fork. "Holy shit," she breathed. "I knew there had to be some reason he wanted to be in Dallas. It's you, isn't it?"

There was a heavy feeling of having misjudged him that was more than balanced out by the hope that she really had been wrong. "Nicole, I have to ask you a few questions and I need straight answers, okay?"

"Of course."

"Did Chris ever tell you we were seeing each other?"

"No."

She watched Nicole closely. The other woman met her gaze evenly. If she was lying, she was very good at it.

"Did you ever ask him for information about Baron Energies?"

"No. Wait, yes, we did speak of it, just once. When I offered him the job."

Oh, God. "Do you remember what was said?"

She nodded. "It wasn't much. I just asked what he'd heard through the grapevine. The press release had just been sent out about your dad, and he asked why I was interested. I think I responded that you'd expressed an interest in alternative energy a few times, but that's it."

Lizzie closed her eyes. She wasn't feeling 100 percent, probably because of her lack of sleep last night and the whole roller coaster of the past few days catching up with her. She really should go home and decompress.

"Are you all right?" Nicole asked, concern in her voice.

Lizzie opened her eyes. "I'm fine," she answered. "Nicole, please be honest here. Did you offer Chris the promotion in order for him to give you information on Baron Energies?"

Nicole's eyes hardened. "You're asking if I bribed him to spy on you, to give me information we could use?"

"Yes, that's exactly what I'm asking."

"First of all, I already told you that I didn't know you guys were even seeing each other. And secondly...if I so much as suggested such a thing to Chris, he'd tell me to stick it up my...you get the picture." She frowned. "If you blamed him for yesterday, you're barking up the wrong tree, sister."

Lizzie believed her. "I had to know for sure," she said quietly.

"Why? Wasn't his word enough?"

Oh, she knew exactly how to make Lizzie feel worse. "It wasn't, no," she admitted. "You've known him a long time?"

Nicole picked up her fork again, looking deliberately nonchalant. "So, the tables are turned, huh? You're going to use me for information about Chris."

Lizzie shifted in her chair. She'd been sitting too long today and her back was aching. "I know. But it's not for professional gain, Nicole. It's... There's a lot at stake."

"You're in love with him."

She nodded. There was no sense denying the truth forever. "We're also expecting a baby."

The blank surprise on Nicole's face would have made her laugh any other time, but not now. "We've only told family so far. But you can see why I'd be a little freaked out if he betrayed me."

Nicole raised an eyebrow. "Or why he'd be freaked out that the woman he cared about and who was carrying his child accused him of something he wasn't guilty of. It all makes sense now."

"What does?"

"I went to visit the local office this morning. Chris gave me his resignation and two weeks' notice."

He'd quit. Why had he done that? Maybe it made sense to Nicole but it wasn't crystal clear in Lizzie's mind. She let out a breath as a cramp rippled across her abdomen. Maybe the cafeteria salad hadn't been a good idea today.

"Will you excuse me for a moment?" she asked, getting up from her chair. "I'll be right back."

She found the public bathroom and stepped into a stall. Her heart began to race when she saw the spotting on her panties. The backache, the cramp, the feeling off... something was wrong. And with the knowledge came a fear so all-encompassing it stole her breath.

She found an old sanitary pad in the zipped pocket of her purse and put it on, then left the stall, pausing to wash her hands before going back to the café. Nicole was still at the table, nibbling at the chocolate pie when Lizzie stopped, not sitting but resting her hands on the back of the chair.

"I'm sorry, but I think I have to go."

Nicole looked up and alarm showed in her eyes. "What's wrong? You look terrible."

"I'm not feeling well. It's…" Her voice broke, embarrassed. "I'm sorry. I think there's something wrong."

She felt suddenly light-headed and began to sway on her feet.

Nicole leaped up and immediately came to her assistance, lowering her into the chair. "You're white as a ghost," she said softly, kneeling beside her. "Is it the baby?"

Lizzie nodded, her eyes blurred by tears now. "Yes. I'm so sorry. This is so unprofessional."

Nicole said an unladylike and definitely unprofessional word and grabbed both their purses. "Forget professional. Let's get you to the hospital. Can you navigate for me?"

Lizzie nodded.

"Let's go then. Can you walk?"

She nodded again. "I'm just…scared." The feeling swamped her again, panic collecting in her chest.

"Well, of course you are. Come on now, let's go." Nicole put a hand under her elbow and led her outside. "My car's over here."

It only took minutes to get to the hospital and Nicole pulled right up to the emergency doors and got out. "Let's get you inside, then I'll park and come in, okay?"

"You don't have to do that. You barely know me…."

Nicole put her hand on Lizzie's. "That baby is Chris's, too, and I happen to think a lot of him. Besides, you shouldn't be alone."

Lizzie walked into the emergency room and was grateful for Nicole's presence as she was triaged by a nurse. When they told her she was being taken to a room right away, she tried to smile at her unexpected friend. "Thank you. For driving me. For staying."

"I'll park the car and come right back."

Lizzie walked through the sliding doors as if in a dream. Minutes later she was dressed in a hospital gown, examined, and a portable ultrasound was brought in. Once the test was done she had to wait, and the curtained-off area offered privacy but no guard against the other sounds of illness around her. She put her hands on her tummy and closed her eyes. "Stay with me, baby," she whispered. "Please stay with me. Your mommy needs you. Your mommy needs to make things right."

In that moment it was just the two of them in the drab cubicle. She remembered taking the pregnancy test and thinking *just flipping wonderful.* Remembered her big plan to tell Chris and get on with things in a very businesslike manner. And none of it had gone the way she'd planned. She'd fallen in love with him instead and then she'd gone and ruined it all. Maybe it wasn't too late. Maybe he could forgive her....

But if she lost the baby, why would he? This baby was the one thread holding them together. "Please don't take my baby," she pleaded softly. "Please."

She pulled her knees in tight, closed her eyes again, and prayed.

"Lizzie?" Nicole's soft voice interrupted her thoughts as she peeked around the curtain. "I thought maybe you didn't want to sit alone, but if you'd rather, that's okay, too."

She could use the distraction. Besides, Nicole had been wonderful considering they were, well, not quite adversaries but not friends either. "I could use the company," she murmured.

"I brought you some water. They said it would be okay." Nicole held out a plastic cup with a bendy straw.

"Thanks," Lizzie answered. Nicole sat in a chair by the bed. She took a sip of the water and since Nicole hadn't asked, offered what little she knew. "They saw me and did an ultrasound, but I don't know anything yet."

Conversation lapsed, and the two sat in silence for a long time. It was odd; Lizzie didn't feel the need to speak and somehow, neither did Nicole. And yet Lizzie was glad the other woman was there. Her impression of Nicole yesterday had been accurate, it seemed. They clicked. It was the damnedest thing.

A nurse popped her head around the curtain. "Lizzie? There's someone in the waiting room for you, but we can only let one person back here at a time."

Lizzie looked at Nicole. "I called Chris," Nicole said. "I figured he'd want to know."

Her throat tightened. "I think I'd like to see him."

Nicole smiled. "Of course. I'll be in the waiting room for a little while longer." She stood and made to leave the curtained area.

"Nicole?" Lizzie looked up at her. "Why did you do this? You didn't have to."

Nicole smiled wistfully. "Because there are times in life that people need help. And sometimes they just need to know there's someone else in the room. Besides, I like you, Lizzie."

She smiled and left, leaving Lizzie only a few moments to prepare herself for seeing Chris.

He came around the edge of the curtain, dressed in his customary dark jeans, boots and a button-down shirt. Her heart jumped at the sight of him and the concern shadowing his face. "Lizzie," he said urgently. "Are you okay? Is the baby okay?"

"I don't know yet," she managed to say, and then to her chagrin, the overwhelming emotions she'd been struggling to hold in came rushing out and she started to cry.

CHRIS IMMEDIATELY SAT on the bed and pulled her into his arms as she wept.

From the moment he'd received Nicole's call until he'd parked the car and run to the hospital doors, his body had been overcome with fear. It hadn't mattered how they left things last night. It didn't matter now that their personal relationship was a mess. He loved her. He knew that. And while becoming a father had been the most terrifying news he'd ever received, learning he might not be after all scared him to death.

"Shh," he soothed. "It's all right. I'm here."

"Oh, Chris," she wept. "I'm so scared. I didn't even want this baby and now I can't imagine not having it. How can that be possible?"

He swallowed against a lump in his throat. He wouldn't cry, too, even though the sound of her anguish was tearing him apart. He'd hold it together, as long as there was still hope. "Because anything is possible when it comes to love," he replied. "It doesn't listen to reason. Don't you know that by now?"

She lifted her tearstained face to his. "No, I don't think that's a lesson I ever learned. And maybe that's why I've failed so badly. Maybe I'd be a terrible mother…."

His heart broke for her. Did she even realize how her mother leaving had marked her so indelibly? "You'll be a wonderful mother," he assured her. "And I'll be right there with you. You don't have to do this alone."

She clung to him, nesting her cheek against his chest. "I'm so glad you're here. I'm so sorry for what I said last night. That I didn't listen. You were right, I was so scared that I'd failed, scared that I'd fallen into the same trap again. Only it was worse because I…"

She broke off suddenly and his heart surged. He knew, as he waited for her to finish her sentence, that they may have come together because of the baby but now it was so much more than that. He'd want to be with her even if there was no child.

"Because why?" he asked gently. "Lizzie." He pressed a light kiss to her hair. "Tell me why."

She shuddered in a breath, pulled away slightly and

lifted her tortured gaze to his. "Because I fell in love with you. That's why it hurt so much."

"But I didn't do what you said."

"I know. I think I knew then, too. And Nicole told me. She thinks a lot of you, you know."

"I fell in love with you, too, Lizzie." The words were out there now and he couldn't take them back. Not that he wanted to, but it was a risk, putting feelings like that out there.

"You did?"

He nodded. "I think there was something profound between us from the start, but the day you met my parents—that sealed the deal for me. I love you, Lizzie. And I'll love you no matter what happens today."

Her lower lip wobbled and he leaned down and kissed it. She tasted sweet and sad, like creamy chocolate and salty tears. Without prompting, she slid over on the hospital bed to make more room. He rested his back against the pillows and opened his arm, making room for her to snuggle in. And that was how they waited for the doctor to return.

It wasn't a long wait; the doctor came back with results of the exams and a smile on his face. "Ms. Baron," he greeted gently as she sat up, pushing away from Chris's embrace. "Hi, I'm Dr. Wade." He held out his hand to Chris and Chris shook it.

"Chris Miller," he said. "I'm the baby's father."

"That is, if…" Lizzie's voice came from the bed, thin and anxious.

"So far, so good. Yes, you're having a bit of spotting, and while a little is normal it definitely needs to be checked out. Your blood work came back fine—your serum hCG levels are still nice and high, and the ultrasound showed the fetus, which at this stage is, oh, about the size of a tangerine."

Chris let out a long breath and looked at Lizzie. Her eyes were shining even though her lip wobbled, probably with the same relief he was feeling.

"That's good news," Chris said, smiling. "What happens next?"

"Well, we'd like to keep you here for twenty-four hours, Lizzie. Monitor you a bit, make sure you don't start bleeding more, that sort of thing. Besides, I think you could use the rest. Your iron's a bit low and rumor has it you have a pretty demanding job."

"Whatever you say," she answered, nodding.

"Good. Now, someone will be along soon to take you up to the ward. Get some rest, okay? And try to relax." He gave an encouraging smile and ducked out again.

"Your family is probably here by now," Chris said, rubbing her arm. "Will you be okay if I go talk to them and then meet you upstairs?"

"You called them?"

"Of course I did. They're your family."

"I hurt you so badly last night, Chris. Nicole told me you resigned."

"We'll talk about all that later. We have tons of time. You just rest, okay?"

She nodded and he kissed her forehead. "I'll see you upstairs really soon."

He made his way back to the waiting room and found Brock and Julieta there, as well as Jet and Daniel pacing anxiously.

"How is she?" Brock asked quickly, looking up from his wheelchair.

"So far everything is okay." Relief swamped him once more, just saying the words. "They're keeping her here for twenty-four hours to be safe."

"I just saw her this morning. Fool girl is working too hard." Brock stared pointedly at Jet.

"She's tougher than you give her credit for," Chris replied. He saw Nicole, sitting away from the family, watching him now but with her phone in her hands. She'd stayed. She really was a good friend. He was sad to resign on the one hand—AB was a good place to work. But it had felt so right, making that decision, that he knew it was time to move on. Make his own life on his own terms.

"Nicole, come on over," he called out, motioning with a hand. "This is Nicole Bennett." He introduced her to the assembled family. "She brought Lizzie in. They were having coffee together."

Julieta shook her hand. "Thank you for staying with her."

"Nicole Bennett from AB Windpower?" Brock looked up at her shrewdly. "You're merger girl."

"I am. I'm also a friend of Chris's."

"So I'd heard," Brock answered. "Thank you. For calling him and shoving those two back together. Wish it were better circumstances, but whatever."

Chris figured he could be knocked over with a feather at that point. He hadn't counted on Brock's support for their relationship. "Nicole, this is Brock, and his wife, Julieta, and Jet and Daniel."

He watched as Nicole shook everyone's hands, but when she came to Daniel, he thought the clasp lasted a little bit longer than the others and a hint of color touched her cheeks. Interesting.

"Are the others coming?" he asked. He got the feeling that the Barons tended to show up *en masse* to a crisis, much like they had when Brock had been injured.

Jet nodded. "Yep. Jacob's on his way back from the job site, Savannah will come as soon as someone relieves her at the store, and we called Carly, although she's home in Houston."

Good. Lizzie wouldn't be alone, especially if he had to run out for a bit. "They're taking her upstairs to the obstetrics ward," he explained. "I've got to run out for a little while, so do you think you could keep her company up there until I get back?"

"Just try to stop us," Daniel said.

"I'd better go, too," Nicole added. "Now that everything's settled down. Tell Lizzie I said goodbye, will you?" She smiled. "I'll walk out with you, Chris."

They stepped out into the sun and walked to the general parking lot. "You have something planned?" she asked him, stopping by her car and searching her purse for keys.

"Yeah. Something." He smiled down at her. "It's time to make things right. I was angry last night and hurt and I walked out rather than fixing things. I need to fix them now."

Nicole put her hand on his arm. "I think Lizzie had to figure a few things out first, too. Don't be too hard on yourself. Keep me posted, will you?"

"I will."

"And forget about going to work tomorrow. Look after your family."

His eyes stung. "Thanks, Nic."

"You got it."

He left her there and went to his truck. He didn't want to be gone long and there was a lot for him to do in a short amount of time.

But one thing was for sure. He was going to make it right. Now that he knew Lizzie loved him, too, everything was within his grasp.

Chapter Sixteen

Lizzie stretched in her bed, waking from a restless sleep. It had taken her a long time to drop off last night. The bed was strange, the sounds were strange, the lighting was strange. If she hadn't been determined to follow doctor's orders to the letter, she might have checked herself out and gone home for the night.

Once she had fallen asleep, she'd had vivid dreams, none of which she could remember now—except for the last one, which featured Chris watching a young boy ride a horse around the arena at Roughneck.

"Good morning," came a soft female voice from beside the bed.

Lizzie scrubbed her eyes and looked over. "Carly! Oh, my gosh, you didn't need to come all this way. I'm fine."

Her sister looked especially young today, in a wrinkled T-shirt and jeans and her hair in two braids instead of one. Lizzie remembered back when Carly was small with cute pigtails that fell to her shoulders. For a while, Lizzie had been the one to put in the elastics until Carly was older and could manage her hair on her own.

"It's not that far. I wanted to make sure you're okay."

"Of course I'm okay. They're taking very good care of us." She put her hand on her tummy.

"I'm glad." Carly came over and sat on the bed. "Can

I get you anything? Water? Juice? Steak and eggs? Dad said your iron's down."

Lizzie laughed. "No. But I'm so glad you're here." She held out her hand, and after a moment Carly took it.

"Me, too."

They were quiet for a few minutes and then Carly spoke up. "Since we were all at the ranch the last time, I've been thinking of Mom."

"I think of her sometimes, too."

"I look at how much you already love your baby and I…I wonder how someone could just walk away from us, you know?"

"I'm not sure we'll ever understand, sweetie."

"Are you still scared about being a bad mom?"

Wow, talk about your hard questions early in the morning. Lizzie rested back against the pillow. "Sometimes. But if I do, I know I'll have lots of help to get through it."

Carly's gaze shifted to an enormous bouquet of flowers on the windowsill. "Are those from Chris?"

Lizzie nodded. Chris had returned last night, bringing her pajamas to wear instead of the hospital shirt, and also her toothbrush and makeup bag, flowers and her favorite fruit-and-yogurt cup from the deli. "It was rocky there for a while, but I think things are going to be all right."

"You really love him, huh?"

Lizzie frowned. "Sweetie? Are you okay?"

Carly smiled back. "Of course. I just… Well, I miss being close by at times like these."

"You could always move back."

Carly laughed, but Lizzie saw something in her eyes that made her worry. Shadows. What was going on with her baby sister?

"I don't think so," Carly replied. "I'm just glad you're okay."

"The doctor scheduled another ultrasound for this morning. If it's all good, and my bleeding has stopped, I'll be good to go home."

"And will that home include Chris?"

There was a knock at the door and the man in question poked his head inside. "Safe to come in?"

"Of course." Lizzie beamed up at him. She still couldn't get over how easily he'd forgiven her. But then, he'd apologized, too, last night, for not talking it through better and walking away instead of staying and working it out.

He'd been so right. About why she held herself back, about her fears. It wasn't until she'd seen him come through the curtain in the emergency room that she truly knew. He had become everything. If she had a hope of being happy, she needed to let go and just have faith.

"I should go for now." Carly stretched out her neck and Lizzie realized that there was a spare blanket on the floor.

"Carly, did you sleep in here last night?"

"Only after about two o'clock." She gave a hesitant smile. "I didn't want you to be alone if anything happened."

Affection for her sister overflowed. "I love you, sis. Thank you."

"That's what I'm here for," Carly replied. "I'm going for coffee. I'll give you guys some privacy."

Chris came in and kissed her briefly. "How'd you sleep?"

"Meh." Lizzie looked up. "Weird dreams. Do you suppose I could get up to use the bathroom? Plus I need to brush my teeth."

"Sure."

She took a few minutes to straighten her hair and splash water on her face. Her breath was minty-fresh but she was pretty unspecial when she looked in the mirror. No makeup, plain ponytail, cotton pajamas. Ugh.

At least the spotting had stopped during the night. When Lizzie came out, her breakfast had arrived and she was happy to have it. Last night she'd been too upset to eat much. As Chris drank his coffee, Lizzie filled up on scrambled eggs, toast and oatmeal.

"I want to talk to you," he said, "but first I want you to drink this. Doc says you need to for your ultrasound today."

She took the bottle of water from his hands and uncapped it. "What do you want to talk to me about?" she asked.

"The future," he replied, and she lowered the bottle.

"I know you resigned your position with AB, Chris. But I know they'll tear it up if you say you're going back. You didn't need to do that to demonstrate anything to me. I was completely in the wrong."

"I don't want to go back."

She met his gaze. He sounded so sure of himself. So confident. "You don't? You're sure?"

"The one good thing about leaving your place the other night was that I had a chance to really think about what I wanted. Me. Not what someone else wanted or expected. I've done that for too long. And I don't want to hurt anyone but at some point I have to live the life I want. And that life does not include running the AB office here in Dallas."

"It doesn't?" Did that mean he was leaving the city, too? God, she hoped not. Not now, when they were just starting to figure out their feelings.

"I'm a rancher at heart. I love the horses. I always have. Working with them would be a dream come true."

"Oh, Chris, I'm so glad." She reached out and found his hand, squeezing it tightly.

"Which brings me to the next thing." He drew in a breath, let it out. "Since I know I love you, and you've said you love me, I was thinking maybe we could stop pretending to be in love and make it the real thing?"

She smiled, feeling a little shy and a whole lot happy. "I think that's a fine idea," she answered.

"I mean really real," he continued, and his expression turned serious. His eyes were dark and beautiful as they looked into hers. The same eyes that had drawn her in that very first night and made her lose herself. Only this time she wasn't as afraid. Only a little.

He reached into his pocket. "Lizzie, I don't want us to just be a couple. I want to make this official, with promises and commitments and a lifetime ahead of us." He held up his hand and she saw the sparkle of a ring between his thumb and finger. "I love you, Lizzie. And I realized yesterday that even if there wasn't a baby I'd love you anyway. I want to be there to hold your hand in the bad times and to laugh with you in the good. I just want you, Lizzie. And whatever life we might build together."

"Oh, Christopher…" She swiped at the tears that clung to her lashes. "Yesterday when everything was going wrong I just wanted you beside me. From the beginning you've been my safe place. I don't know how or why but I looked at you and things clicked into place, so quickly it was terrifying. I thought I'd ruined it forever."

"Not even close," he murmured. "Will you marry me, Lizzie? And let us make a home for our baby?"

She nodded and held out her hand. He slid the ring on it and then gathered her in his arms. They held each other for a long time, taking strength from each other, giving love and acceptance.

Eventually they sat back, and he held her in his arms, much as he had the previous afternoon. "I was thinking," he mused, "that we might put in an offer on that ranch close to Roughneck. You'd be close to your family and the commute isn't too bad."

Excitement fluttered in her heart. "The colonial with the pillars? It's beautiful."

"I'd like to work with rodeo stock." He gave a shrug. "I was thinking of talking to your brothers and dad about some options and the possibility of partnering up to use the arena. What do you think?"

"I think it sounds perfect." Not only that, but there was a satisfaction and enthusiasm in his voice that she loved to hear.

There was a discreet knock at the door and a technician stood in the entryway with a rolling machine. "It's time for your ultrasound, Ms. Baron."

She nodded, giving an emotional sniff and looking down at the ring, a perfect square-cut diamond set in platinum. She was going to be a wife and mother—two roles she couldn't have imagined even six months ago and now was looking forward to rather impatiently.

Chris moved to the other side of the bed while the technician set up, and then they both watched as she used the wand to scan Lizzie's uterus.

"There you are." The wand pressed deeper in one spot and the technician clicked some buttons on the machine. Lizzie tried to crane her neck around but the tech moved the wand. "I promise I'll let you see, I just need to get some data first," she said with a smile. "Is this your first ultrasound?"

Chris nodded. "Yes. Well, except for yesterday's in

the emergency room. We weren't sure we'd be able to see anything. Scary."

The tech smiled again. "Well, there is definitely a baby, no worries there." She clicked a few more buttons and it seemed to Lizzie that it took forever. Finally she swiveled the machine a little. "Okay, Mom and Dad. Here's your little one."

She worked the wand a bit, trying to get the best picture, and then suddenly Lizzie saw it. A perfectly formed head with a button nose, the torso, arms and legs. Inside her. As they were watching and marveling, the baby moved, and the technician laughed. "Playing hard to get," she joked, and taking her time, she scanned again until they got a perfect picture of a delicately arched spine.

"Your doctor will be in to talk to you later, but you can rest easy. Your baby is still snug as a bug in there."

"Can we get pictures?" Lizzie asked, knowing she'd want to preserve this moment forever.

"Of course." She handed Lizzie some tissues so she could wipe off the gel.

The pictures came back before the doctor arrived, and Lizzie and Chris snuggled together on the bed, looking at them.

"That's our baby," she whispered, wondering if she'd ever felt this happy before in her life.

"Our family," Chris corrected. "That's what we are, Lizzie. Family. For always."

She twisted around and kissed him until she heard a throat clear from the direction of the hallway. She looked up and grinned. The whole family was there. All her brothers and sisters, her dad, Julieta, even Anna and Alex. For so long she'd felt alone. The one who had to take care of everyone else. Right now, though, they were all here for her, and their love and concern went straight to her heart.

She looked at Chris and saw all the love she'd ever need in his eyes, and then she nodded. "You'd better all come in," she said. "We have news."

* * * * *

Be sure to look for the next book in the
TEXAS RODEO BARONS *miniseries!*
Follow the family saga in Trish Milburn's book:
THE TEXAN'S COWGIRL BRIDE
Available from Harlequin American Romance
in July 2014!

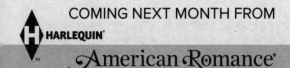

COMING NEXT MONTH FROM

HARLEQUIN®

American Romance®

Available July 1, 2014

#1505 THE REBEL COWBOY'S QUADRUPLETS
Bridesmaids Creek
by Tina Leonard
Cowboy Justin Morant is on the rodeo circuit looking for success—not a family. But when he meets Mackenzie Harper and her four baby girls, he realizes this may be the real gold buckle he's after!

#1506 THE TEXAN'S COWGIRL BRIDE
Texas Rodeo Barons
by Trish Milburn
Savannah Baron needs to find her mother, so she turns to P.I. Travis Shepard. During their search, Savannah and Travis grow closer, but falling in love was never part of the arrangement!

#1507 RUNAWAY LONE STAR BRIDE
McCabe Multiples
by Cathy Gillen Thacker
When Hart Sanders discovers he's a father, he wants to create a stable, loving home for his eighteen-month-old baby boy. But is turning to runaway bride Maggie McCabe the right thing...or will she run again?

#1508 MORE THAN A COWBOY
Reckless, Arizona
by Cathy McDavid
Liberty Beckett and Deacon McCrea have a chance for a serious relationship...but how can they take it when Deacon agrees to represent Liberty's father in a fierce legal battle that divides the entire Beckett family?

REQUEST YOUR FREE BOOKS!
2 FREE NOVELS PLUS 2 FREE GIFTS!

HARLEQUIN

American ★ Romance®

LOVE, HOME & HAPPINESS

YES! Please send me 2 FREE Harlequin® American Romance® novels and my 2 FREE gifts (gifts are worth about $10). After receiving them, if I don't wish to receive any more books, I can return the shipping statement marked "cancel." If I don't cancel, I will receive 4 brand-new novels every month and be billed just $4.74 per book in the U.S. or $5.24 per book in Canada. That's a savings of at least 14% off the cover price! It's quite a bargain! Shipping and handling is just 50¢ per book in the U.S. and 75¢ per book in Canada.* I understand that accepting the 2 free books and gifts places me under no obligation to buy anything. I can always return a shipment and cancel at any time. Even if I never buy another book, the two free books and gifts are mine to keep forever.

154/354 HDN F4YN

Name _____ (PLEASE PRINT) _____

Address _____ Apt. #

City _____ State/Prov. _____ Zip/Postal Code

Signature (if under 18, a parent or guardian must sign)

Mail to the **Harlequin® Reader Service:**
IN U.S.A.: P.O. Box 1867, Buffalo, NY 14240-1867
IN CANADA: P.O. Box 609, Fort Erie, Ontario L2A 5X3

Want to try two free books from another line?
Call 1-800-873-8635 or visit www.ReaderService.com.

* Terms and prices subject to change without notice. Prices do not include applicable taxes. Sales tax applicable in N.Y. Canadian residents will be charged applicable taxes. Offer not valid in Quebec. This offer is limited to one order per household. Not valid for current subscribers to Harlequin American Romance books. All orders subject to credit approval. Credit or debit balances in a customer's account(s) may be offset by any other outstanding balance owed by or to the customer. Please allow 4 to 6 weeks for delivery. Offer available while quantities last.

Your Privacy—The Harlequin® Reader Service is committed to protecting your privacy. Our Privacy Policy is available online at www.ReaderService.com or upon request from the Harlequin Reader Service.

We make a portion of our mailing list available to reputable third parties that offer products we believe may interest you. If you prefer that we not exchange your name with third parties, or if you wish to clarify or modify your communication preferences, please visit us at www.ReaderService.com/consumerchoice or write to us at Harlequin Reader Service Preference Service, P.O. Box 9062, Buffalo, NY 14269. Include your complete name and address.

HARI3R

SPECIAL EXCERPT FROM

 HARLEQUIN®

American Romance®

*Welcome to **BRIDESMAIDS CREEK**,*
Tina Leonard's new miniseries featuring wild, hunky
cowboys and adorable babies.

Read on for an excerpt from
THE REBEL COWBOY'S QUADRUPLETS
by New York Times *bestselling author Tina Leonard.*

"Can I help you?"

"I'm looking for Mackenzie Hawthorne. My name's Justin Morant."

"I'm Mackenzie."

Pink lips smiled at him, brown eyes sparkled, and he drew back a little, astonished by how darling she was smiling at him like that. Like he was some kind of hero who'd just rolled up on his white steed.

And damn, he was driving a white truck.

Which was kind of funny, if you appreciated irony, and right now, he felt like he was living it.

Sudden baby wails caught his attention, and hers, too.

"Come on in," she said. "You'll have to excuse me for just a moment. But make yourself at home in the kitchen. There's tea on the counter, and Mrs. Harper's put together a lovely chicken salad. After I feed the babies, we can talk about what kind of work you're looking for."

The tiny brunette disappeared, allowing him a better look at blue jeans that accentuated her curves.

Damn Ty for pulling this prank on him. His buddy was probably laughing his fool ass off right about now, knowing how Justin felt about settling down and family ties in general. Justin was a loner, at least in spirit. He had lots of friends on the circuit, and he was from a huge family. He had three brothers, all as independent as he was, except for J.T., who liked to stay close to the family and the neighborhood he'd grown up in.

Justin was going to continue to ride alone.

Mrs. Harper smiled at him as he took a barstool at the wide kitchen island. "Welcome, Justin."

"Thank you," he replied, not about to let himself feel welcome. He needed to get out of here as fast as possible. This place was a honey trap of food and good intentions.

He needed a job, but not this job. And the last thing he wanted to do was work for a woman with soft doe eyes and a place that was teetering on becoming unmanageable. From the little he'd seen, there was a lot to do. He had a bum knee and a bad feeling about this, and no desire to be around children.

On the other hand, it couldn't hurt to help out for a week, maybe two, tops. Could it?

Look for THE REBEL COWBOY'S QUADRUPLETS,
the first story in the BRIDESMAIDS CREEK miniseries
by USA TODAY bestselling author Tina Leonard, from
Harlequin® American Romance®.
Available July 2014, wherever books and ebooks are sold.

American Romance®

Love or family loyalty?

Liberty Beckett was so used to watching longtime crush
Deacon McCrea ride at her family's Reckless, Arizona, arena,
she nearly forgot the handsome cowboy was an attorney.
But it won't be hard to remember now that Deacon is
representing Liberty's father in the legal battle dividing the
Beckett clan and threatening the Easy Money Rodeo Arena.

This case is Deacon's chance to clear his name in Reckless.
He didn't anticipate the powerful effect Liberty would have
on him. Their attraction is undeniable…and a huge conflict
of interest. To save his career and Liberty's relationship with
her family, Deacon knows he needs to avoid Liberty.
But what a man needs and what he wants are two very
different things….

Look for
More Than a Cowboy
by *New York Times* bestselling author
CATHY MCDAVID,
the first title in the
Reckless, Arizona miniseries.

Available July 2014 from Harlequin® American Romance®.

www.Harlequin.com

HAR75529